The situation amazed Lissa. Here she was, in her nightclothes, striking a wager, extending her hand to a gentleman who looked as if she'd backed him against the wall. "So you won't shake my hand, Max?"

Again his gaze darkened. "No, my dear," he said, his voice suddenly soft. "I'd say these special circumstances call for an equally special seal to our bargain."

Taking her outstretched hand in a large and firm grip, Max pulled Lissa toward him. She could feel the heat of the fire from behind him. It kindled his eyes and warmed his breath before his lips touched hers.

Lissa allowed his mouth to linger for only a moment, and then she stepped back. Here was a new game she didn't know how to play.

"Remember, Damalis," he whispered, releasing her hand, but still looking into her eyes, "winner names the spoils."

The Reluctant Bridegroom

Sally Martin

JOVE BOOKS, NEW YORK

THE RELUCTANT BRIDEGROOM

A Jove Book / published by arrangement with
the author

PRINTING HISTORY
Jove edition / October 1991

ISBN: 0-515-10686-0

Jove Books are published by The Berkley Publishing Group,
200 Madison Avenue, New York, New York 10016.
The name "JOVE" and the "J" logo
are trademarks belonging to Jove Publications, Inc.

PRINTED IN THE UNITED STATES OF AMERICA

10 9 8 7 6 5 4 3 2 1

For Larry

And for Lauri, Holly and Julie

I love you

The
Reluctant
Bridegroom

♋ *Chapter One*

WHEN SHE WAS perturbed, Lady Agatha Westmane wasn't above pulling childish faces. Though she was nearly three-score years, and though she was the daughter of a duke as well as the sister to another didn't matter a jot.

And what was the cause of her present unladylike expression? An aging Pekingese perched on her niece's lap. As her ladyship watched Lissa fed him another bit of cake from the tea tray. Puck's watery, pop-eyes stared back at Aggie.

"Spoilt creature," Aggie muttered, plucking up her late brother's quizzing glass.

Both ladies were seated in the painted parlor of West-mane House which was on the north side of Piccadilly. But while Lissa sat on a formal sofa, Aggie was at a gilded, Kentian desk with an enormous sheet of wickedly scrawled parchment stretched before her. Although this chamber had been decorated in the grand manner by Kent himself, Aggie preferred the smaller parlor with its smaller scale.

"Did you say something, Aunt Aggie?"

Agatha looked up from the paper again, this time her features suitably schooled. "I said, that these lines and tiny names on this family tree are making me quite dizzy. It's no wonder it took the College of Arms almost a year to untangle the mess. For all of these relations, there are few of us left. And those few are so distantly related."

"Are you saying you can't see any reason for Lord Stinton having lost out to this . . . this soldier?"

Lissa's voice rang with disapproval, a disapproval that caused the elder woman to hesitate before replying. She wished she could soften her niece's starchy ways—to show her how much of a stick . . . No. Aggie could hardly bear to think it, much less say it. But it was true that at seven and twenty, her darling niece had all the airs of a spinster. And her disapproval of this particular soldier seemed especially strong.

"The truth is I am inclined to admire Maxmilian," Aggie finally said.

Lissa looked aghast. Straightening on the ornate sofa, she assisted the dog to the carpet and swept the lap of her lavender gown free of crumbs. "You *admire* him?"

"Everything we've heard from the solicitors involved in this odious succession business has been quite favorable."

"But . . . but he's a common soldier."

"Not so common. He's a cavalry officer. From all reports, he's one of Uxbridge's finest."

"But . . . he . . ."

"His father was an Oxford don, my dear," Aggie said gently. "At the age of eighteen, Maxmilian bought his colors. And he has made colonel. A very young colonel. He's widely traveled, and—"

Understanding sprang into Lissa's delft-blue eyes. "I know what you're saying. You admire him because he's led an adventurous life. You always admire adventurous people, and this . . . this soldier has lived unconventionally for the last sixteen years. He's lived from pillar to post, from India to Spain to . . . to heaven knows where, picking up heaven knows what uncouth habits. He can hardly be a fit successor to Uncle."

Lissa rose from the sofa, clearly agitated.

She began to pace, to further press her point. "If Maxmilian Jameson is such a *fine* gentleman, why haven't we heard from him? He hasn't written us a line! Uncle Gervase would never have been so lacking in consideration . . . so . . . so rag-mannered for all his aloofness. The least this *fine* son of an Oxford don could do is to put his household and his very relations—no matter how distant and *insignificant*—on notice of his arrival."

Aggie didn't counter her stream of sharply uttered words. The poor girl was worried; worried about not only the shocking change in the succession, but about their futures as well. After all, for the past several years their lives had been so set.

That her bachelor brother, Lissa's uncle, would die seemed inconceivable. Gervase had been so perfectly suited to his station that it seemed impossible for him to die. Then when he did, Aggie and Lissa had assumed Viscount Stinton would inherit and their lives would continue unchanged. Viscount Stinton was as much fixed at his country estate as they were in London.

And now their world had changed, especially Lissa's. Though technically her uncle's ward, Lissa had been running Westmane House since before her come-out. Because Agatha had never liked dealing with menus, linen inventories, and especially not household accounts, Lissa had taken on these duties like a duck to water.

It was such a pity, Aggie thought, studying her niece. The girl now stood before a window. The April light lit her hair, and it shone in a soft, red-gold nimbus. Her profile revealed a straight little nose and perfect complexion. While Lissa had never been called an Incomparable—because of that softly red hair that was unfashionable—she was definitely patrician and certainly charming.

If only she weren't so prim, and growing primmer every day. Aggie remembered the lively girl who had once lurked beneath that somber pose. Hadn't her Lissa been the most delightful child? Oh, yes, Lissa had been as bright as the morning. But, alas, Lissa, like Aggie herself, had lost a first love tragically. That occurrence had marked the beginning of Lissa's long decline into an unreachable sobriety.

"Additionally," Lissa said, turning abruptly from the window, "I can't understand how you can call this man by his Christian name. You speak of him as if you're close acquaintances when he may toss us out on our ears."

"Why, Lissa. When have you ever used a cant phrase like 'toss one out on one's ear'?" Aggie took a lighter tack. "As I say, dear, I feel free to call Colonel Jameson Maxmilian because I admire him." She smiled. "In any case, I have the most wonderful expectations of the man."

This time Lissa surprised Aggie. A reluctant smile transformed her classical features. "Oh, Auntie," she said, bending to give Agatha's cheek a quick kiss. "You're still a dreamer."

Before the younger woman could move away, Lady Agatha caught her niece's hand. "And while you may deny it, my girl, your dreams are still there inside of you, too."

Lissa's smile disappeared. "I gave up on dreams a long time ago, Aunt." While she spoke softly, her small frame stiffened as she headed for the door. "Please don't mind if I leave Puck with you for a minute. I must check with Pinkerton on Hardy's employment at Sandford House."

"But isn't Hardy our own footman?"

Lissa paused at the ornate doorcase. "I dare say, Aunt. I don't know what to do. After fourteen months of living in retirement, I think it's ridiculous to keep a large staff. We don't entertain anymore, at least not on the grand scale to which we were accustomed. I'm gradually letting people go. Pinkerton and I are finding places for whom we can."

Her aunt nodded but didn't pursue the subject. "Aren't you promised to Lord Palmer for an afternoon drive?"

"He sent a note around saying he's afraid that he might be catching another cold. After being so red and sore, his nose is only now regaining its normal shade."

Aggie suppressed an unladylike snort. The manner in which Lord Palmer had to-doed over his last cold had been ridiculous, but typical of the man. Still, Aggie knew better than to comment. She didn't want her niece to become an antidote like herself. Even Boysen Palmer would be better than no husband at all. She looked over at the damnable Pekingese, who now snored in a splash of sunlight on the Turkey carpet. The idea of Lissa ending up with only a snappish beasty for companionship forced her ladyship to voice a question that had been troubling her for weeks.

"Has Lord Palmer come up to scratch, my dear?"

Lissa hesitated, her fingers on the loose doorhandle. "Speaking of cant phrases, Aunt . . ." she said, rattling the handle as an evasion.

"Don't start pulling hairs with me, my girl. If I've had the temerity to ask, surely you can answer me squarely. After all, he's been showing his face around here for nearly three years."

Lissa lifted large, bright-blue eyes to meet Aggie's waiting gaze. "I've told Boysen I need time to consider the matter. It's such an important decision, and . . ."

Aggie managed to hold her tongue, but just barely. Grasping the quizzing glass, she went back to the papers. A strand of faded, red hair escaped the confines of her lace cap.

"I'm sure you'll do what's best, dear. You always do."

Out in the second-story passage, Lissa smoothed the skirts of her conservative lavender gown. Half-mourning.

While they continued in half-mourning, she and Aunt had ordered colors for the spring season. She tried not to think about what this season could bring.

The great house rested quiet and familiar. It comforted her. As she glided toward the grand staircase, it enfolded her. Usually, as she dealt with household tasks she tripped up and down the several rear staircases. But today she needed the peace of the house to seep into her bones.

She didn't know what the next few months would bring. She was almost certain she would refuse Palmer. But what then? Should they go on as always? Should she and Aggie consider setting up on their own? When would the new head of the family arrive? Surely, she and Aunt should, at the least, remain at Westmane House to welcome him—to hand over the keys, so to speak.

The grand staircase led down to the main entrance of the house. It had been one of the first mahogany staircases to be installed in London, and during the day, the soft light of the windows illuminated the large bronze standing at the bottom. According to tradition, William Kent had chosen this statue of a graceful nude gladiator as the focal point for the impressive entry.

Of course, the naked gladiator was considered shocking, especially when compared to the otherwise very conservative manse. Lissa had seen many ladies avert her eyes rather than look at him. Even so, she liked him perhaps best of all the treasures of the house.

And to her, he didn't seem so shocking. After all he did wear that wonderful helmet, as well as a drapery which fell across his broad shoulders and along an outstretched arm. He wasn't so very scandalous . . . As she perched on tiptoe and ran her finger across his shoulder someone rapped on the door sharply.

Lissa froze. She was unable to think what to do. A lady

never answered her own door, but Pinkerton was nowhere in sight.

And then, the door knocker sounded again, reverberating throughout the stairwell. The caller was clearly impatient. Lissa had just decided to open the door herself, when the door banged open.

She watched half in horror as the most powerful male she'd ever seen strode in. He wore a blue coat with blazing gold braid strung across the chest and along the cuffs. The heavy trunk he carried on his shoulder explained his impatience.

While Lissa observed him with a mix of awe and umbrage, he hefted the trunk to the floor, turning to slam the door he'd left standing open. She still stood frozen. She knew who he was and he wasn't at all in the style of Westmane. He was her worst nightmare come to life.

The new duke strode to the doors that led into the State Drawing Room. Those, too, he swung wide. Lissa prepared herself to finally give a frosty greeting when he spoke.

"Heigh ho!" he called out, pacing the marble flooring to the doors which opened off the other side into yet another state room. "Damnation," he muttered.

At last, swinging around, he spied her, standing a few risers above the entry floor. Their eyes locked. Oh, no. He wasn't at all in the style of Westmane. His hair ran riot in deep chestnut waves. The tan lines in his face emphasized his look of determination, and never before had Lissa seen a day's growth of beard. Nor had she ever experienced such a sudden breathlessness at the sight of a man.

Although he seemed as startled as Lissa felt, he spoke first. "I beg your pardon about the door. My trunk is . . . well, it's deuced heavy." His sudden smile transformed his face and lit his sherry-colored eyes. "I'm Max Jameson, ma'am."

"So I should hope," Lissa replied, unable to smile, to think, or to breathe.

He smiled even more broadly. "I'm unaccustomed to London ways, of course, but am I asking too much by requesting your name?"

Unconsciously, Lissa straightened her shoulders. "I am Damalis Westmane. I'm your . . . your . . . well, I suppose we're some sort of cousins."

He still smiled maddeningly. "Cousins, eh? I didn't know I had a cousin. How delightful."

While Lissa had never in her adult life been teased, she had the vague suspicion that this man—this infuriatingly crude man, with his unabashedly unshaven face—was making a May game of her.

"Beg pardon, again, ma'am, but did you say Damalis?"

"Yes. I am niece to the late Westmane. My father was the second son of the house."

Even to her own ears, she sounded as if she were lauding her position over him. But he had confounded her with that . . . that easy smile.

"You must excuse me for staring," he said, "but you're somehow familiar to me."

"I suppose that's because I have the typical coloring and look of a Westmane." Again she sounded prim, even to her own ears. She knew she was the patrician Westmane he was not, and yet the differences didn't seem to bother him a rap.

"But I've never clapped eyes on any of the Westmanes before," he replied, sounding puzzled. He turned from her to the bronze gladiator. "My, my, and who's this fine fellow?"

As he halted just before the statue, Lissa had the oddest sense that like was meeting like. She also fought down a hot flush. Of course, the face of the Roman gladiator stretched smooth while Colonel Jameson's face bore the signs of his past—a past filled with male adventure and experience.

Either fortunately or unfortunately—Lissa didn't know which—an explanation of the gladiator was made unnecessary. Puck had escaped the painted parlor and headed pell mell, down the staircase past her skirts, his silky red fur flying. Hurdling himself toward the newcomer's not-so-shiny boots, he barked and spun and yelped.

"Puck!" Lissa called to the dog, mortified. But to no avail. Her hand claps, together with his barking, raised a veritable din that echoed through the stairwell. For a moment the colonel simply stood where he was, his eyes rather amusedly tracking first the advance and then the retreat of the little dog. Puck's behavior had never shamed Lissa more. Nor had her dignity ever been so crushed. Her lavender skirts flying, she made a very unladylike attempt to pick the dog up.

As Puck squirmed away her nightmare deepened. Here she was, meeting the new duke, looking and sounding like a shrew. She closed her eyes, praying for the earth to swallow her.

Just then, the colonel stamped a booted foot on the marble floor. "That's enough, old boy," he called out.

The large entry fell silent. For a moment the dog froze on the spot. His eyes looked about to pop from his head. Then with a final yap, he dashed around Lissa and back up the stairs. The pair that remained peered at each other.

The colonel's eyes shone warm with amusement. But before Lissa could think of what to say, Pinkerton came into the entry via the green baize door that lead to the nether regions of the house. "So sorry, miss," he said, sounding unusually harried. "There's someone at the stables claiming to be—"

"Yes," said the colonel, stepping forward. "That would

be my batman, Bagley. He's seeing to my horses. We've dismissed the cart we hired for the baggage. What's your name, my fellow?"

" 'Tis . . . 'tis Pinkerton, sir."

The colonel gave him one of his ready smiles. "And I'm . . . well, I'm Westmane, my good man."

"Yes, sir. I mean . . . yes, Your Grace." Then as if he were addressing Lissa's Uncle Gervase instead of a travel-stained soldier, the butler straightened his black coat and bowed in his grandest manner. "If you will come with me, Your Grace, I'll have a bath brought abovestairs."

"You have it precisely right, Pinkerton. It won't do for a duke to stand about in his travel dirt."

As Pinkerton began the long ascent to the next story, His Grace paused to look at Lissa. His smile was softly personal. Lissa wondered if he weren't roasting her again.

"Thank you, my dear cousin," he said, "for the welcome. I've never had a homecoming, and you and your equally red-haired companion have made me feel most welcome."

Confused, Lissa watched as he pivoted away from her and started up the staircase in the butler's wake. Her eyes followed the sway of his broad shoulders, took in the blatant claim of his uniform.

Oh no, there was no refinement in either feature or body. Nothing about this man defined him the style of Westmane. He was everything a gentleman of fashion was not, and yet he was undoubtedly the most fascinating male she'd ever encountered.

Rousing herself, Lissa gathered her dignity and went along to the kitchen without looking back. She would not allow herself to gape at him like some common type. And in the days to come, she knew that many would surely gape.

🍂 Chapter Two

LISSA AND AUNT sat in the grand State Drawing Room. If Lissa had been a cat, her tail would have twitched smugly. Though she'd been thrown off guard at first, she was now in her element. When Maxmilian Jameson had sent word downstairs that he wished to present himself to Lady Agatha for a short informal meeting before he went out to dinner and they continued on with their own evening schedule, Lissa had planned her attack.

Mustering her forces, she'd chosen her gown and her jewels with the same care she'd shown in selecting her battle position. She wanted to impress upon him just how unlike the preceding Westmanes he was. And what better place for showing him the grandness of the family than this equally grand space which represented the epitome of William Kent's brilliant architectural design?

Red cut silk hung the walls and echoed in the upholstery. Baroque rang in the moldings and in the excessive carving of the furniture. Gilded architectural motifs sang in every detail. Yes, this was all that was Westmane. It was everything Maxmilian Jameson was not.

"Bless me," Aunt Aggie said, sighing. "I can't remember the last time I sat in here. It's always so overwhelming, don't you think?" she asked, not really expecting a reply.

Her aunt was ensconced in a weighty armchair that matched the one where Lissa was perched. There were several more chairs, circling about the enormous fireplace. Even with the large fire Lissa felt the chill.

"And these jewels," Aggie said, "I can't imagine why you insisted on wearing them. Maxmilian will think we go on like this regularly."

"Well Aunt," Lissa said, trying to distract her ladyship. "His Grace should be introduced properly. He should have at least one chance to see what his family is about."

"Goodness, this isn't what we're about. At least, not since Gervase is gone. Oh, I know my brother enjoyed the pomp and show. And though you stood by his side through all the folderol as I recollect, you didn't enjoy it much, either."

The great clock in the corner sounded the hour, saving Lissa a reply. Right on schedule, the doors were swung wide by liveried servants, and in walked none other than the mouse for Lissa's trap.

Of course, he didn't much look like a mouse. For a moment, Lissa faltered. On seeing his advance across the carpets, she had that same catchy, breathless sensation she'd experienced when she'd first seen him in the entry. Still, she called up her courage. He was hovering over Aunt Aggie's hand, quite properly bowing.

Disappointed, Lissa realized his blue uniform was equal to the room. He looked like a courtier come to pay his addresses; his formal cavalry gear was also brilliant and baroque and excessive. Gold braid and buttons, gold fringe on his shoulders, even great gold tassels swinging from his wrapped waist, looked designed with the room in mind.

"My Lady Westmane," he said. "How good it is to meet you." His slow, easy smile put up Lissa's back.

"We've waited a long time to meet you, Your Grace," she said, also smiling.

"Indeed, we have," Lissa heard in her own disapproving tones. "Your Grace," she amended.

"Ahhh." His smile broadened to a grin as he focused his golden eyes on Lissa. "Cousin," he added warmly.

"Oh, no," Aggie declared. "I don't think we're at all closely related. Surely not enough to call one another cousin. I spent most of my afternoon examining the family tree and there's hardly any connection at all."

"Only enough to call me to my duty," he replied, this time something other than warmth showed briefly in his eyes.

Lissa was aghast. His comment implied that he might be disappointed with his new title. Surely that wasn't possible. Surely any man—even a soldier—would rather be a duke.

"Pray, Your Grace," Aggie was saying, "you must sit down. I know it's very uncomfortable in here, but Lissa insisted—"

Lissa broke in. "Pray, do sit down . . . Your Grace."

His gaze met hers again. He seemed to read her every thought, perhaps even her intentions. Still, he smiled graciously. "I'm sorry I can't stay for long. Some old military friends asked that I dine with them when they heard I'd arrived. I'm afraid I don't know anyone else in London."

"Oh, but we'll be happy to remedy that, Your Grace." Aggie chuckled. "Lissa and I are putting off our blacks and going out into society again. You must come along with us."

Lissa remained silent. Surely her aunt should have waited for an invitation to stay before making such an offer.

Maxmilian went on as if all had been decided. "I should like that. But I'm afraid I don't have much experience with the ladies—with tea cups and that sort of thing. And then, I have these horribly large fingers."

Again Aggie laughed. "I must admit that we won't be able to do much about your fingers, but Lissa and I will be more than happy to help otherwise. Won't we, Lissa dear?" she added, looking toward Lissa.

"I'm sure that any number of people will want to meet you . . . Your Grace." Lissa couldn't seem to say "Your Grace" without stumbling over it. She knew the colonel noted that fact.

His smile was sweet. Too sweet. "Surely, if we're to jog along easily, you'll call me something other than Your Grace. Indeed, I'd feel more comfortable if you would. Since my first name is equally daunting, perhaps you'll call me Max. My friends do, and if we can't be cousins, I hope we can be friends."

"Well, I for one shall enjoy calling you Max," Agatha enthused. "The question is, what will you call me? As I say, I'm hardly your aunt. And while I'm certain everyone will be shocked if you call me Agatha, you surely must."

Another smile, this time a genuine one. "Agatha, it is. At least, in private. And you, Miss Westmane?" he inquired, his smile more cautious. "What shall it be between us?"

He'd thrown down the gauntlet. "I suppose Christian names will do."

"Good. Damalis, then."

"My stars," Aggie said. "I haven't heard 'Damalis' used since her poor mama died. She always called Lissa, Damalis. But then, my love," she added, turning to her niece, "you wouldn't recall that." She looked back at their new relation. "Shortly after she was born, Lissa's parents were drowned on a rough crossing from Paris. Poor child. She came to live with my brother and me, right here at Westmane House. And, except for summer holidays in

Oxfordshire with her maternal grandparents, she's been here ever since. Although the Westmane seat is in Derbyshire, we never go there. Bowwood. I suppose you've been hearing about Bowwood."

"Actually, I haven't heard too much," the duke said. "I've been traveling from one place to another on the continent, and any communications have had a hard time keeping up with me."

Lissa saw light spring into her aunt's eyes. Her aunt had longed for adventure in her own life. "I daresay, you've been almost anywhere one can imagine."

He chuckled. "I must admit that I've been a lot of places. My style of travel wouldn't suit anyone but myself, however."

"And this past year? Where is it you've been?"

The light in his eyes dimmed. "I'm afraid I can't say where I've been. I *can* tell you, however, that I was connected to Wellington's staff. From that, I'm sure you can deduce much. What with Old Boney's escape from Elba and the Congress of Vienna declaring him an outlaw to be stopped at all costs, there are fireworks ahead."

"Oh, goodness," Agatha said. "I dislike even thinking about it. We had believed it was all over."

"Indeed, we did," he murmured. "Indeed, we did."

So that was it, Lissa thought. He'd been called from a duty he loved, to one that would deny him his life of adventure. Suddenly she felt sorry. Sorry for him, sorry for the situation, sorry for the way she'd acted.

But he was smiling again, taking Agatha's hand in his own and bending over it. "I must bid you good evening, my dear lady. Although I doubt we'll run across one another easily in this grand old house, I hope we can talk again sometime soon. I hope to see you when the will is read at the beginning of next week."

"Oh, yes. We've been informed of that," Aggie agreed. "And then, my wish is to put these past fourteen months behind us and to go on more happily."

"Just so," Max averred. Turning to Lissa, he took her hand as well. "And to you, my dear Damalis, I wish a good evening."

Before she could reply or voice an apology, he turned and strode out. Lissa watched the sway of his broad back. She had to admit he looked decidedly handsome. He'd met the room with a confidence that had diminished neither it nor himself. While past Westmanes would have blended in, would have taken their places with an elegant formality, his sense of ease had left the room to itself. He'd won her respect.

After he'd gone, Lissa and her aunt had one of the evenings that had become typical over the last year. Boysen, with his sore nose and possible relapse, sent a note saying he'd have to excuse himself from dinner and the cards the trio had planned. Not that Lissa minded so much. Even though it appeared as if she and her and were entirely welcome to remain at Westmane House, she was restless. Oh, she was grateful that at least those worries had been relieved. But the restlessness continued to plague her, though just what it was that bothered her, she couldn't say.

Oddly enough, Lissa felt better by the next morning. The day dawned as one of those soft, first days of spring which encouraged thoughts of even warmer hours ahead. Although Boysen remained too unwell for one of their regular carriage drives, Lissa coaxed Aunt into their own chaise. They had a wonderful time, too, as they drove through the nearer parks.

The next few days went smoothly. Lissa's concerns, the old restlessness, receded further from her mind. She also acknowledged a growing curiosity about her new family member. While she didn't see him, or even hear much about him except through Aggie, she thought of him more than she liked to admit.

Since her habit was to drink her morning chocolate in bed, her appearance at the breakfast table, which the duke now regularly shared with her aunt, would seem too obvious. In any event, she had to wonder what he thought of her. She'd treated him very badly, both upon his arrival, and particularly on that following evening in the State Drawing Room. She was a bit embarrassed to face him again, and waited for events to bring them together, which she knew they would. They were soon to gather for the reading of the will, and following that, she hoped to start over again.

And then it was upon them—the day the will was to be read. Lissa joined Aunt Aggie and the new duke in her uncle's former study. As could be expected, Lord Stinton didn't come up from the country, and as unlikely as it seemed, there was no one else even remotely involved.

Lissa's first surprise was seeing the new duke in Corinthian day garb. While she would have thought him too Vulcan-like for the more graceful attire of a gentleman, she had to admit he looked quite dashing. He'd obviously found one of the finest male clothiers in London, because his blue coat fit his broad shoulders to perfection and his buff pantaloons clung to the length of his powerful legs as they should.

The single fault was his neckcloth. It was clear that his large fingers weren't practiced at tying fanciful knots, and his batman was evidently accustomed to only military stocks.

As Lissa came in last, His Grace smiled at her. When he took her elbow, she felt suddenly shy. "Miss Westmane, please meet Mr. Wilson, of Buckles, Buckles and Wilson."

"Your eternal servant, miss," the elderly man replied.

Moving about, the three family members each took one of the old-fashioned carved chairs. Mr. Wilson sat behind the desk. Lissa couldn't help noticing the oversized portrait of her Uncle Gervase above him. After all this time, he looked both foreign and familiar. At least he didn't seem the be-all and end-all of Westmane anymore.

As Mr. Wilson started to read the long formal document in a dull, droning voice, Lissa had everything she could do to concentrate on what the balding man was saying without falling asleep. She also watched Aunt Aggie's hand uncurl and relax on her skirts. She feared her aunt might doze off and tumble from her chair.

Her hardest task, however, was keeping her gaze from the new duke. He sat in a beam of light, directly across from her, and her eyes never left him for long. He was concentrating, of course. She noticed that he was both at ease and yet alert: a sharp combination of contrasts. She saw how faded scars marked his large hands: a faint line marred his jawline, another interrupted one of his chestnut-colored eyebrows. And yet, there was something entirely civilized about him. Something comforting, even. His powerful body spoke of his rough and ready past. And yet, from what Aggie said, he was adapting to London life very well.

Oh, yes, he'd occupied himself with more than a mindless, brutish calling in the years gone by. Additionally, he had an obvious intelligence with which to meet the years ahead. She knew she would be watching with interest as he evolved into a true Westmane.

But Lissa had other thoughts to fend off. She'd never before, in her seven and twenty years, contemplated the manner in which a man was made. Sitting across from her as he was, she slipped easily into comparing him, as she had at first, with the gladiator in the entry hall. Naturally, some of those comparisons brought a blush to her cheeks, and—

"What?"

Maxmilian Jameson was out of his chair, advancing on the smaller, older Mr. Wilson at the desk.

Lissa didn't know what had happened. She only knew enough to reach a reassuring hand to her aunt. Lady Agatha barely escaped falling off her chair.

"I'm sorry, Your Grace," Mr. Wilson was saying, "but I'm afraid it's quite true. This will can only reflect what your man of affairs has told me. It seems the duchy is on the brink of impoverishment. Your two predecessors spent so little time on estate matters, while expending so much money, that your coffers are almost empty. Every estate is mortgaged to the hilt. Several are on the brink of foreclosure. The Westmane seat in Derbyshire is the worst off of all your properties. Bowwood hasn't been visited by a Westmane for the last twenty years. The tenantry there is dispirited and unproductive. Indeed, Your Grace, absentee landlordism serves no one well. Only this house remains free of debt. It, together with its collections, were paid for long ago, and from what your man of affairs tells me, the seventh duke kept it free and clear so as to avoid gossip. Everything else, however, will have to go under the gavel to keep even this much solvent. And what you will use for future revenues, if you are to stay on here, I cannot imagine."

Silence fell on the room. Lissa's head swam. Agatha also appeared awash.

"Well, well, well," Max finally muttered.

"The best answer for you, Your Grace," the solicitor said, "is the usual one."

Max's voice sounded surprisingly even. "You will leave everything with me, Mr. Wilson. Especially, the account books from the man of affairs. I intend a careful examination. But before you go," he added, "what is this 'usual answer' to which you refer?"

This brought the busy fellow up short, a sheaf of papers in his fist. "Why marriage, Your Grace. With your title and connections, together with this house and its collections, you should be able to make the match you need to bring the estate into solvency. It's the only solution, Your Grace."

Max assumed his most soldierly stance and manner. "No matter what it seems I may have become, my good sir, I am no gazetted fortune hunter."

"But . . . but, Your Grace." The solicitor couldn't put his papers away quickly enough now. Still, he endeavored to smooth things as best he could. "No . . . no one would think that. A marriage of convenience is the traditional, yes, even the *accepted* solution for your situation. An alliance with another great family will be expected. I assure you, there's no dishonor in such a union. Why, they've been the mainstay of the Westmanes. How else do you think a large duchy is made?"

The solicitor reached both the end of his packing up and his speech at the same time. Without further ado, he excused himself and the room fell silent again. Silent, that was, until Max let out a softly muttered oath. He realized then that Lissa and Aunt Agatha stood behind him, clutching one another for support.

"I beg your pardon, ladies," he said.

"It's quite all right, Max dear," Agatha replied.

Lissa noticed their shared breakfasts were putting them on easy footing. Aggie showed no reluctance to go on.

"Mr. Wilson is right, dear Max. You must marry. Gervase should have married an heiress long ago. I never understood why he didn't."

"It's obvious that, if he could ignore the financial

demands of the duchy, he could also discount any other obligations. No disrespect intended."

"Well, yes," Aggie said. "But never fear. Between us, we can set it right. And then, there are Lissa's probable connections, as well."

Max's eyes pierced Aggie's. "What does Damalis have to do with this?"

"Well, I—" Her ladyship faltered as she never did. "I might be rushing my fences, but—"

"What Auntie is trying to say," Lissa heard herself explain, "is that I've had an offer."

His eyes remained intense. "One you've accepted?"

"One I'm considering."

"Well, don't think you have to fall into parson's mouse-trap for my benefit."

"Don't worry about Lissa, Max," Aggie insisted. "For now we'll concentrate on you. It will be easy. Lissa and I can draw up a list of eligible young ladies this very afternoon. What with the season getting underway and our excellent connections—"

"I beg your pardon, Aggie," he said, interrupting, "but I'm head of this family now. I'll speak for us and for our futures. And by that, I mean all of us. There's bound to be an answer in those papers, and I intend to find it this side of being leg-shackled."

ℰ *Chapter Three*

Ever since Lissa and her fiancé had been overturned in a one-horse buggy, she'd been terrified of small, open carriages. She'd watched her intended die on that afternoon, and she'd never forgotten. This also meant she would never climb into a curricle, no matter how fine. Even watching a phaeton, particularly a high-perch one, maneuvering by, gave her the shivers.

Fortunately, her friends took her aversion into consideration, and Boysen Palmer was extremely considerate. In the wintertime, he often found himself either looking for a chaperone for a closed chaise on a cold day, or calling up his mother's antiquated barouche on a merely chill one.

In fact, Lissa and Boysen enjoyed jaunting about the environs of London so well that they drove out as often as possible. Depending, that was, upon the weather, the available carriage or chaperone, and Boysen's proclivity for taking cold.

On the day following the reading of the will, his lordship sent a note to Westmane House, requesting that Lissa accompany him on a drive along the old highway toward Oxford. He was feeling much better, and decided it was time he ventured out. There were wonderful views to be had around and about Ealing, and he hoped they could enjoy them again. They could revisit St. Mary's Church, that interesting little sixteenth-century parish church in the tiny village of Twyford. He said, in his note, that he felt totally recovered. He assured Lissa that she need not worry that it was largely overcast and a bit dank—he felt fit for the afternoon.

Thinking that his note sounded more cheerful than he had in over a week, Lissa considered her reply carefully. She didn't want to go, especially not after the day before. But turning his note over in her fingers, she sent along a neat acceptance. She hoped to feel differently by that afternoon.

By the appointed hour, however, she still didn't feel enthusiastic. Nor did seeing Boysen's choice in equipage help. Despite its pile of lap robes, and the certain thoughtful addition of hot bricks, the old barouche pulling into the curved drive below her bedchamber window looked cold and uncomfortable. What she usually saw as a treat, even on a cool afternoon, loomed ahead as an obligation.

Turning back to her waiting dresser, Lissa called for her warmest pelisse and her fox wraps. Puck remained where he was in his favorite spot on her bed, ears twitching.

"Yes, Miss Westmane," the dresser said, more a respectful retainer than a personal body servant, who'd been with Lissa for years and years.

Lissa decided that fox looked well with the Titian shade of her hair, and even while its trim wasn't considered the height of fashion, she liked the play of color in the pelts. Boysen, looking recovered, seemed delighted at her appearance in the painted parlor, and after a few words with Aggie, he escorted Lissa down the grand staircase. Beyond the portal, two horses, two drivers, and a single footman waited with the open carriage.

"I feel it's been forever since we've seen one another," Boysen said, helping the footman tuck Lissa into the carriage robes. "You look quite a treat, my dear Lissa."

Lissa smiled weakly as the bone-rattler, as she thought of it, swayed and pulled off with a jar. Making an effort, she smiled more brightly at her companion. Boysen was very nice, and she was determined to be nice in return. She would also enjoy their spin in the countryside. The breeze against her cheeks felt invigorating, and once they escaped the tight, noisy traffic of London's streets, she did begin to feel better.

But finally, the silence grew strained. And while Lissa would have preferred to sit quietly and absorb the sense of freedom, she knew she had to broach the subject that caused the strain. After all, the scandal over the reversal in the Westmane fortunes would have to be faced.

"I suppose you've heard our news," she ventured.

Looking at her, Boysen smiled that pale smile of his. In fact, everything about him was pale. Not to say that he wasn't nice looking. He was. He was tall and slender, and his clothes fit him as the vogue required. His hair, although receding, was a light blond, and his eyes a light grey. He was conservative and conscientious, and also very much attached to London and its society. Just as Lissa had been at one time.

"I'm very sorry, my dear Lissa."

For a moment, Lissa thought Boysen might reach over and pat her gloved hand with his gloved hand. But he didn't. He was invariably a gentleman. Despite the sensitivity she could sometimes read in his eyes, he never touched her unless in accord with strict propriety.

"Actually," she said, "it's very kind of you to be seen with me so soon. You could have waited until things settled down somewhat. I would have understood."

"No. Now, Lissa, don't say that." Boysen could be determined when he wanted to be. "No one sees any of this as your doing. It's his former Grace who'll bear the back of the brush for this affair. And rightly so. Who would have thought?"

"Indeed, who would have thought? We had absolutely no idea. Hearing the will yesterday was like . . . well, I suppose it can be compared to taking a physical blow."

"I can imagine. I can imagine," he lamented. "My poor, poor Lissa."

Lissa returned her gaze to the awakening landscape. Somehow, this wasn't helping. She only felt all the more aggravated, and she wanted to spare Boysen the heated feelings he would see in her eyes.

"And what's to be done, now?" he asked, after a moment.

"I don't know."

"Surely, the new Westmane will take things in hand."

"Oh, he's done that. From what Aunt Aggie says, he's been closeted in the library with my uncle's man of affairs since we heard the news. I doubt there's much to be done, though." Another moment passed. Lissa watched the steady breeze divide the bright fur of her muff, much as a dresser makes a neat part to the scalp. "Have you met him, yet?"

"The new duke, you mean?"

"Yes. I thought you might have run across him. He's out every night. He's yet to have dinner at home. In fact, I never see him."

"No, I haven't met him. I've heard about him, but I haven't seen him."

"And what have you heard? I mean, what's the opinion aside from my uncle's horrible doings?"

"Well, this morning, at least, everyone is placing the blame where it rests. Precisely how his new Grace will come out of it, though, is hard to predict. I suppose the question is, how much money is left?"

"Just so. And that's obviously what he's looking into."

"Of course, he still has the title, and that will take him far. A name like Westmane will stand him in good stead no matter what. Well, almost no matter what. If he can marry quickly enough and well enough, this is sure to pass."

"But what have you heard of him personally?"

"Well, we don't exactly run in the same circles, you know. And then, I've been tied to my bed. But from what I've heard, he's the military type we expected. He keeps mostly to male company—dines at the Guards. He's already up for membership at White's. And Boodles. If he has such obviously staunch male friends, both in and out of the military, the clubs will be interested."

"And this scandal won't hurt him?"

"Truly, Lissa dear, you can answer that as well as I can." Palmer looked as if he were losing interest. "There are variables involved. But in the end, he can come 'round. It all depends on what 'papa' is looking to buy a title. Who do you think, of the season's debs, craves to be a duchess?"

"Oh, no," Lissa said, distaste unexpectedly filling her mouth like brass. "I won't play that game. In any event, he says he won't marry for money."

Boysen's laugh was as pale as his coloring. "It's the only way he'll come about. You must tell him so, Lissa. He might not know."

Lissa examined her long-time companion. His nose shone pink. And his ear lobes, too. His skin was too fair for the cool air, and he appeared blotchy. She looked back at the scenery. "When is your mama coming up for the season?" she asked to change the subject.

"Actually, I don't think she will. She despises London, you know."

"And your sisters?"

"I hardly think either one of them will make the effort, not with one being in the family way and the other recovering from the same condition." He paused. "Look here, Lissa," he said, "about this scandal business. About the uncertainty. My proposal remains as firm as ever. In fact, it might be a good idea to declare ourselves, and at the end of the season, go quietly off to my seat and be married."

Lissa could not look at Boysen now. She didn't know why his inability to brave the out-of-doors and retain his good looks bothered her. It made her feel petty. And then, this talk of marriage always unsettled her.

"Thank you, Boysen. You are too kind to stand by me. But, if I were to desert Westmane House now, things would appear worse than ever. If I were to leave, I couldn't live with myself. The new duke deserves whatever countenance I can lend him."

Boysen smiled his thin smile. "You're a good 'un, Lissa dear. For the present, I'll understand. But not for long."

Lissa forced herself to return his smile. But she felt oddly desperate. She also regretted coming out with him. The afternoon was hardly underway, and she wanted to go home.

By the time Boysen helped her out of the old barouche at Westmane House, Lissa's nerves were in tatters.

"I can see, Lissa dear, that you are sadly out of curl," Boysen said. "What with the scandal breaking, I can sympathize. I don't suppose you will attend Lady Paley's ball tonight. Her Ladyship is firing off her second daughter."

Lissa paused at the entry. As usual, the few servants were out of earshot, and they had a private moment to speak. Only the gladiator overheard.

"I really should attend the ball. I should go, and hold my head high, and . . . But no," she said, more softly. "I won't go."

"I think it better that you don't." His tone was serious and confidential. "Let it all die down somewhat. Most everyone thinks you're still in mourning, at any rate."

Lissa nodded. She'd had enough. She watched Boysen walk stiffly down the steps, climb into his barouche and disappear around the drive. As the front door closed behind her, the word "Coward" rang as an inner accusation. For so long being a Westmane had made her feel important. She'd been proud to stand next to her uncle in the receiving lines, to serve as his hostess, to be introduced as his niece. Although, outside of evenings spent in society, she'd hardly seen him. And now it seemed a sham. He'd been no more than a hoax. In truth Lissa didn't know what to think of him, of their position, of anything.

After a brief nap, Lissa dined with her aunt before they settled in to play cards. The new duke, Aggie told her happily, had finally emerged from the library and left for the evening. Aggie seemed confident that all would be put to rights.

Less optimistic than her aunt, Lissa had a restless night. Following an hour of tossing, she donned her finely worked wrapper, put on her fancy slippers, and tossed her long, red-gold braid over a shoulder. Her restlessness had set her frilly nightcap askew, and she righted that by the light of the candle she carried to the glass.

Since sconces were burning in the passageways, Lissa was sure the new duke hadn't returned yet. This enabled her to leave a dozing Puck and make her way to the library without fear of running into either the duke or anyone else in the halls. Down the grand staircase she swept, candle flickering, as quiet as a mouse. Passing the gladiator, who looked especially fierce in the half-light, she went along the final corridor to the library.

Lissa loved the library at Westmane House. It was decorated in a grand style—the library furniture, in particular, expressing William Kent at his most fanciful. But best of all, Westmane House had a wonderful collection of books, including everything from Aunt's shelf of travel books, and even the parody of that literature, *Dr. Syntax in Search of the Picturesque*, to plays, to novels.

Lissa noticed that the new duke's desk was piled high with papers while a nearby table supported numerous large ledgers. Sympathy burst upon Lissa. This fine man had returned to England to do his duty, only to find that duty onerous and embarrassing.

Lissa drifted to the desk. The candles that glowed there beckoned to her. Surely, she should blow them out, she thought, before spying a small volume topping the neat stack of papers.

Curiosity overwhelmed her conscience, and she picked up the calf-bound volume. It was very worn, and even more surprisingly, printed in Greek. Aeschylus's *Agamemnon*. She'd known that Max's father had been a teacher of the classics, but Max didn't seem the type to read such fare. Opening the inner cover, she saw it was inscribed in a precise script: *Maxmilian Alexander George Jameson*.

Flipping through the pages, she found translations of various words and phrases noted in the margins. Those were executed in the same bold hand that matched the scrawl on the papers below. Max had done the notations. Max Jameson was the translator of the ancient Greek play.

Here was another proof of Lissa's false pretensions. She'd assumed he'd turned away from his scholarly background. She'd even thought he'd probably run off because he'd been unable to appreciate the more refined life his father had led. She was beginning to feel as disgusted with herself as she was with her Uncle Gervase. How and when had she become so . . . so . . . ?

A sudden sound brought Lissa up short. With a guilty flush, she put the book down. She looked over to the hearth where the remains of a fire glowed. She couldn't see much else. Once again, an unlikely curiosity coaxed her in that direction, and the nearer she came, the more she could make out.

The sleeve of a corbeau-colored coat draped the armrest of a very large chair. The hand that fell over the gilded wood was square and battle-scarred.

Caution advised Lissa to retreat to her room, but she didn't. She was too curious. And while she also admitted to a certain amount of fascination with this man—a fascination she excused on the grounds of his being a type that was new to her—tonight's curiosity was mixed with something else.

Again, she endeavored to see him in the same light as, say, when Aunt Aggie had shown her a frog in a bottle or explained mushrooms and fairy rings. But somehow, none of that worked. Thoughts of what was proper, and what was not, didn't apply, either. At least, she couldn't make them apply.

This very masculine man mesmerized her. His relaxed hand, the way his chestnut hair fell into unruly but somehow appealing waves, the sun-tipped lashes that now screened his remarkable eyes from her, the smile that spread naturally across his lips . . .

Well, heavens, she told herself. She stood over where he'd fallen asleep in a chair. She was in her night things and he was minus his cravat. Her changed circumstances seemed to be unraveling her sensibilities. Straightening her shoulders, she turned from the chair to leave without choosing a book.

"I must be dreaming," he said.

When she paused, Lissa's night things swirled about her like the most delicate ballgown.

A smile touched his lips. "I hope I don't wake up."

"You *are* awake," she said crisply.

"If I'm awake, then what are you doing here in your nightclothes?"

"This is a library. I came for a book."

His sleepy eyes drifted down to where her hands grasped one another in front of her. "You came for a book?" He sounded purposefully doubtful. "I was hoping you'd come to dance in my dreams."

"I'll be leaving now, Your Grace."

"No, I'll be good. I promise," he added, straightening in the chair and sounding more himself. "I apologize. I'm a bit overtired. Don't worry, I'm not cup-shot."

"I thought you might be working on—" A wave of Lissa's hand indicated the piles of ledgers and papers behind her.

"No. I've had to sound retreat on that front. The news is as bad as we've heard. And as irreversible."

Once again, Lissa felt a twinge of sympathy. Some of the stiffness drained out of her face and shoulders.

"In truth, my dear," he added, "I'm afraid I have some rather worse news for you." Rising from the chair, he motioned that she should take it, while he moved to stir the fire. "That chair's warmer so, pray, sit down. I would've waited until tomorrow, but maybe it's just as well we talk before I tell Aggie."

Lissa perched on the edge of the chair, nervous. How could there be more? When he turned from the renewed blaze, its light flickering on his corbeau-colored cutaway coat, on the subtle stripes in his waistcoat, he again urged her to be more comfortable.

She sank into the chair's surprising warmth. He positioned himself before the large hearth. Lissa watched him closely as he searched for his words. "It seems your Uncle Gervase not only ruined the estate, but freely dipped into the funds you and Aggie were left by your father and her father respectively."

"What?" Lissa felt her pulse begin to thud in her throat. Here was a blow she hadn't thought to expect. Nor, she was sure, had her aunt.

"I'm so sorry," he said softly. "When we discovered the evidence, I could hardly believe it. The man must have been a scoundrel."

"But . . . what's the extent of the problem?"

He sighed deeply.

"Oh, pray. You must tell me."

"You and Aggie are in a position much like mine. While I have some money of my own put by, you have some as well. But the hard fact is, that I must do something now in order to secure our futures. While I take full responsibility for us all, and I certainly won't touch what you and Aggie have left, I also realize I must act quickly. And, to that end, I must enlist your help."

Lissa grasped for cogency. "My . . . my help?"

"Yesterday, that deuced lawyer suggested I marry. As you'll recall, I balked at the suggestion. The last long hours, however, have taught me differently. And while I would prefer not to marry, I no longer see myself as merely fortune hunting. In fact, I must look at this as my friends have encouraged me to look at it. What I have left is a title. A title that will earn me an alliance. And while I may find this concept personally degrading and distasteful, I've been assured it's not shameful. I have, in a word, Damalis, come around to the practicalities."

Sympathy welled up in Lissa, as it had before. And again, it was mixed with something else. She did, in fact, admire him. How many men of her acquaintance would have taken a like situation and handled it with such good cheer and common sense?

"Yes, Your Grace, I'll help you. And I know Aggie will, too. While most of my friends are setting up their nurseries, Aggie has a wide circle of acquaintances with daughters. She'll do you the most good."

"Fine. And as to Aggie, what do you say to not telling her about this other business unless we have to?"

"I also agree on that count, Your Grace."

And then, it finally came—that wonderful smile which lit his sherry-colored eyes and softened his features. "I see you're now able to 'Your Grace' me without it sticking in your throat."

Lissa flushed and looked at where her hands lay clasped against the delicate embroidery of her wrapper. "As to that evening in the State Drawing Room, Your Grace, you must forgive me. I would have asked your pardon sooner, only—"

"Don't continue along those lines, please. What I need now is an ally—a friend. I need someone who can teach me the ways of society."

Lissa lifted her clear blue eyes to his shining gaze. "I'll be pleased to be your ally, Maxmilian."

"Max."

"Max."

"Good! And it's done. But then, one more matter. About this engagement you say you're considering. When you make your decision, you're to think of nothing except pleasing yourself. You're not to worry about the money. When this gentleman is ready to talk finances, we'll be better situated, and we'll . . . well, we'll take that step when we're ready."

"Yes, Your Gr— I mean, Max."

Max locked his hands behind his back and rocked slightly on the heels of his evening shoes. "I can't tell you how much better this is. I feel as if I've finally taken a grip on things."

Lissa smiled. "You do realize that what we're setting out to accomplish is not easily done, even without the time element involved?"

"Let's see, now. It's the second week in April and—"

"And the season peters out as the summer comes on."

"Oh." The amber of his eyes darkened somewhat.

Lissa smiled dryly. "Yes."

"Well, let's put a frame around it, then. Set a goal, so to speak. A goal will keep me oriented."

"All right. But again, I warn you. To contract a marriage within the span of a season will be difficult. A union that will get you the funds you need, one that won't be . . . well . . ."

"I understand. Crass. But even an engagement, *a short one*, will do."

"Still, great families don't rush into these matters."

"Not unless they have their own reasons for rushing."

"True. But how are we to know the motives of others?"

"They'll know mine. And then, I'd rather hoped that you . . ."

Lissa laughed, surprising herself. "No, not I. It's Aggie who'll be our best resource in this. And she'll also be delighted to test her mettle."

"So then, let's set a date."

"Well, anything past July will be beyond likelihood."

"Then let's say mid-June. How about June eighteenth? That was my mother's birthday. That should be a favorable date."

"All right. June eighteenth."

"I wish I could wager on this with one of my friends. It

would give me an incentive. But I dare not add grist to the gossip mills."

"But you say we're to be friends. Why not wager with me?" Lissa, who didn't even wager at Silver Loo, as Aggie did, couldn't believe her own ears.

"But you're supposed to be on my side."

"And I am. But that doesn't mean I think it's likely we'll succeed in what we hope to accomplish."

Max appeared doubtful. "But how can you wager against me and help me at the same time?"

"Just because I'm a female, doesn't mean I can't think impartially. While my heart hopes you win, my head remains cool enough to be cautious."

Max smiled broadly. His eyes danced. "By Jupiter. I think I've chosen myself the best ally, the best friend, I can."

Lissa's laughter joined his, echoing in the large room.

"And what are we wagering, my dear?" he asked.

Lissa was nonplussed.

"It can't be money," he said, eyeing her knowingly.

"No." She screwed up her nose distastefully. "Money isn't fun."

"Then, you name it."

"But, but I'm at a loss."

"All right, then, winner names the spoils."

Lissa stood, the layers of fine, embroidered fabric settling about her, her red-gold braid hanging heavily on her shoulder. "Winner names the spoils," she repeated levelly, walking toward him with her hand held out.

In this case, it was he who looked a bit starchy. "So we are to shake hands?"

"Isn't that the custom?"

"Among gentlemen."

"Not among friends?"

"I'd say with friends of the same sex, perhaps. But of opposite sexes, no. With a gentleman and a lady, definitely no."

The situation amazed Lissa. Here she was, in her nightclothes, striking a wager, extending her hand to a gentleman who looked as if she'd backed him against the wall. It was a heady experience. Surely, it was his sherry-colored eyes. They'd intoxicated her. "So you won't shake my hand, Max?"

Again his gaze darkened. His smile even slipped. "No, my dear," he said, his voice suddenly soft. "I'd say these special circumstances call for an equally special seal to our bargain."

Taking her outstretched hand in a large and firm grip Max pulled Lissa toward him. She could feel the heat of the fire from behind him. Heat also emanated from his grasp. It burned in her cheeks. It kindled his eyes and warmed his breath before his lips touched hers.

Lissa allowed his mouth to linger for only a moment, and then she stepped back.

"Remember, Damalis," he whispered, releasing her hand, but still looking into her eyes, "winner names the spoils."

ᕬ *Chapter Four*

A PREVIOUS DUCHESS at Westmane House had disliked the style of Kent. Lissa often thought it fortunate her tenure had been brief. As it was, this duchess, who had lived in Paris just before the Revolution, had dismantled only a few rooms: Her own suite and a breakfast parlor that was tucked away on the first floor had been done in the French manner.

The transformations made for a lighter, airier change, and Aunt Aggie invariably took her meals in the breakfast room. Lissa knew she could find her there—together with Max—on almost any morning. Find them there, that was, if she could muster the courage to face Max.

The previous night she hadn't closed her eyes. Nor had she been able to read. Her meeting with Max in the library had been unique in her life, and not only because she'd ignored the proprieties. After all, they'd discussed the most serious news she'd ever heard. She and Aunt were on the verge of destitution. And yet, the round of Lissa's thought centered on Max's kiss.

Not that she hadn't been kissed before. Her intended had stolen kisses in the exuberance of their youth and with every expectation of marrying one day. Boysen had kissed her on two occasions in the past three years, but those advances had been awkward and brief.

Max's kiss had been confident. It had been a revelation. One she wished she could forget. And she'd just as soon forget that improper wager she'd made with him, too. In her practical way she decided she'd been unbalanced by the threat of poverty, and that given time, she would put it all in perspective.

And that brought her to this morning, to the doors of the breakfast parlor. She straightened her shoulders and lifted her chin. She'd promised Max she would help him find a duchess, and she was honor bound to do that. Much lay ahead of them, and finding him an heiress would also ensure that she and Aunt were also settled.

Her chin held high, Lissa swung into the breakfast parlor. Three surprised faces met her: Max's cleanly shaven one, Aggie's familiar features, and Pinkerton's impassive mask. The table had been cleared, and the butler was pouring the last of the coffee into Max's cup. Aggie sat, scratching out her awful scrawl on a piece of paper between them.

"Why, Lissa, love," her aunt called, "are you feeling quite the thing?"

"Right as a trivet, Aunt." Looking Max in the eye, Lissa said, "Good morning, Max," firmly and impersonally.

"Good morning." While his face remained impassive, his eyes examined her closely.

"Will you have breakfast, miss?" the butler inquired.

"No, thank you, Pinkerton. Just the usual hot chocolate."

"I'll fetch it, miss."

Lissa sat down across from Max and next to Aggie. Her eyes tried to decipher her aunt's messy scrawl. "And who have you listed?" she asked.

"Well . . ." Aggie replied, her smudged fingers pulling at one of her faded red curls. "It's rather daunting. More daunting than I would have thought. You and I know," she added, with an arched brow, "the ladies who would fall into his hands at the merest nod. But we also know *why* they'd fall so easily. I'm speaking of Lady Baird, who is entirely out of the question."

Avoiding Max's eyes, Lissa murmured that Lady Baird was definitely out of the question. Pinkerton was delivering her chocolate, and while his presence would never deter her aunt, he had the discretion to let himself quietly out.

"And then," Aggie said, "there's Miss Relph. She's been on the shelf for these four years past. Sir Robert is rich enough, heaven knows. And he's certainly willing enough to get the chit off his hands. But if that talk—in Miss Relph's come-out season, you recall, Lissa—about the stable lad . . ." Lissa glimpsed the light in Max's eyes, while Aggie plunged on. "Well, I don't—"

"No," Lissa said. "Miss Relph is not quite the thing. Who else?"

"Lady Hatchbull is firing off her daughter this very next week. We have the invitation card. I haven't seen the gel, but . . . well, Aurora Maypost says she's pudding-faced and fubsy. Poor dear. Of course, Lady Hatchbull is enormously rich and generous to a fault. She'll do well by her Sapphire. It's more that Max should have someone pretty to look at across the breakfast table. And all the Hatchbulls tend to be either pudding-faced, or butter-toothed, or . . ."

Max spoke solemnly, though an unholy light shone in his eyes. "Sitting with the pair of you, I'm convinced that it is, indeed, imperative to meet a pretty face come the light of day."

"There!" Aggie agreed, smiling at his compliment. "*No*. It's *no* to Sapphire Hatchbull," she declared, scratching off what seemed to amount to that name on the list.

Lissa was now determined to avoid Max's eyes. Aggie

pressed on. "Mr. David Dow's daughter is recently wid-
owed. She's worth considering, but she's still in blacks.
And then, Max might have to go to Northumbria, and we
don't have the time or money to waste on trips that might
not do us any good."

Aggie's eyes scanned the list. "And while Miss Pindling
has the sweetest manners, for I've met her several times
myself in the company of her cousin, Horace, her papa is a
Cit. I, personally, wouldn't care a rap about that. However,
the leap to duchess is quite a leap to make. Everyone would
say so, and some would even shun her. That could be
uncomfortable."

Lissa glanced at Max. Although he listened with every
intent, she could see he barely contained himself.

"The Glendinning gel will also be shot off this year. But,
my stars, what with her uncle and father and brother,
gaming runs rampant amongst the Glendinnings. Max
would have to keep the cards under lock and key. And, of
course, a like madness taints the blood of the Askeys. Lissa
dear, I realize you quite like Glynis Askey. But we all
know, no matter how much Lady Askey insists it's otherwise, that her brother-in-law, poor creature, is kept at
Askey Towers, behind barred windows." Aggie shuddered
visibly. "We cannot take a chance on an alliance like that."

When Aggie lapsed into silence, Lissa heard her own
sigh. She dared not look at Max again. "I see what you
mean. It's more complicated than I would have thought."

"Perhaps," Max said, "we shouldn't be so particular.
Maybe I should just get out there and get my feet wet, so to
speak."

"Heavens," Aggie said. "Unless you have several seasons, that will never do. If you're to form a connection by
June . . . what was the date?"

"June eighteenth," he replied, nodding wickedly at Lissa.

"What about Miss Barlworth?" Lissa said, ignoring him. "I hear she's very intelligent, and makes charming conversation."

"Well, I suppose. If Max doesn't mind spots."

"Look," said Max, sober for the first time. "I'm not expecting to fall in love. While I'm perfectly willing to woo the gel and to do the pretty by her, the objective is not to please myself. I'm resigned to the facts, here. I must marry, and the union will be an alliance tied up with banknotes and a title. I'll be a pattern card of propriety to my duchess. I'll make every effort to jog along in the most peaceable manner. But she'll be as much awake on all counts as the rest of us."

"We know that, dear," Aggie agreed. "It would be nice, however, to have some romance, to have some . . . some . . . After all, you'll be marrying for the rest of your life."

"Aggie," he said, firmly. "I'm pockets to let. I can't afford romance. In any case, I'd rather be honest with this lady. I'd prefer no emotional ties, at all."

"But . . . but . . ." Aunt floundered. "That's positively gothic."

"It's also, as I've been told, the norm."

"But it doesn't have to be that way for you. Surely, we can salvage something from this. Something just for you."

Reaching over, Max patted her ink-stained fingers. "Aggie," he said, "I wouldn't recognize love if it hit me with a barge pole. My experience has deadened me to the niceties of life. In fact," he said, recovering his usual light address, "Lissa has promised to polish off my rough edges. I only wish she could help Bagley with my cravats."

Max's teasing coaxed Aggie into a smile. But before

Lissa could suggest another name, the door to the small, more lightly furnished parlor, opened.

"Lord Palmer," Pinkerton announced, closing the door again.

"I hope you don't mind that I had myself announced," Boysen said, as if he hadn't been having himself announced for years. "It's just that it's such a lovely day. I thought Lissa and I might drive out to Havering. Havering has high land and open country with splendid views. We could stop at the Golden Lion at Romford. A wonderful little place— sixteenth century. Good morning, My Lady," he added, bowing over Aggie's hand. "I know you dislike carriage drives above all things, but perhaps you might like to join us simply because it's such a fine day."

"No, thank you, Lord Palmer," Aggie said.

Boysen smiled a pale smile, moving on to pick up Lissa's hand. "Good morning, my dear. I hope you will say yes."

Lissa realized Max was watching with interest, and she flushed. She couldn't help comparing Boysen's cool kisses, his cool coloring, to Max's vibrance. Max was alive with a male experience and a masculine intelligence that escaped the rank and file of *tonnish* gentlemen.

When Lissa saw Boysen's eyes on Aggie's mess of quill and paper and ink pot, she used his distraction as an excuse for avoiding his invitation. "We've been discussing possible matches for my cousin," she said, hoping her use of "cousin" would explain their informality. "Lord Westmane, this is Lord Palmer." A moment later, she realized with mortification she shouldn't have admitted such a calculating conversation.

The men exchanged greetings. Lissa was tongue-tied.

"I say," Boysen said, "what a dashed shame to be brought to such a pass, Your Grace."

As a well-to-grass baron, Boysen oversaw his responsibilities with every consideration. His policies were invariably conservative, and yet in step with the times. He was the most eligible *parti*.

"Yes," admitted Max. "My position is rather uncomfortable. But, as you see, I've enlisted the best help."

"Come to think of it," Boysen said, "what about Daphne Huntley? I daresay you've considered her."

"Daphne Huntley!" Aunt exclaimed. "My stars. My wits have gone begging. I had a letter from her grandmama this Christmas past. She mentioned that Daphne would be coming out this year. The Huntleys have seven daughters to get rid of." Aggie's eyes brightened as she ticked off the needed particulars. "Lord Huntley is as rich as Croesus, and everyone knows he's sworn to have titles for each girl. The first is a countess, a Scottish title you know, but the second and the third . . . oh, dear, I can't recall. It seems to me as if the third came away from her season with no more than a gentleman of the untitled aristocracy from somewhere near Newcastle."

"Yes, I recollect," Boysen said. "Old Huntley was most disappointed. He says visits to Newcastle are abominably cold."

"Maybe Derbyshire will appeal to old Huntley," Max said with a glint in his eye. Lissa was sure the glint was directed at her.

Boysen, who was sadly lacking in humor, peered at Max, puzzled. "Bowwood is in Derbyshire," Max elaborated, "perhaps, Lord Huntley will find the idea of visiting Derbyshire appealing enough to . . . er . . ."

"Oh, I see," Boysen said, nodding and forcing a pale smile. "Yes, yes, I see."

For all Max's claim of being ignorant of the refinements, Lissa could tell he found the *ton*'s reasons for marrying distasteful. Dictums and dictates she'd lived with all her life

seemed suddenly ridiculous. People should marry, for . . .
what? She wasn't ready to answer that, so she caught up
with the ongoing conversation.

"I'd really appreciate that," Max was saying.

"Oh, it will be no inconvenience. My man, Pinseat, has
a delicate hand with cravats. We'll come around, say
tomorrow morning?"

"Tomorrow morning will be fine."

"Good. Have your batman press a generous three dozen,
and I'll bring along a few myself."

"I appreciate it," Max repeated. "And thank you, too, for
suggesting Miss Huntley."

"Her papa could certainly set you up right and tight."

"That's true," Aggie said slowly. "My concern is the
time. And then, it's such a shame poor Max has to marry at
all. Not when he doesn't want to. Wouldn't it be wonderful
if we could find Old Mad Jack's treasure?"

Lady Agatha's eyes shone. She had a side which longed
for adventure, a side that had filled Lissa's young head with
stories, stories that had no true basis in reality.

"What treasure is this?" Max asked. "Is it connected with
the duchy?"

"Oh, indeed," Aggie said, off on her favorite tangent.
Lissa sat back on her chair, trying to catch Max's eye while
Boysen stood politely by.

"Now," Aggie stated as a preamble, "you must not
worry. Mad Jack was the single Duke of Westmane to ever
be queer in the attic, and he had no children to pass along
his madness. No one is sure what unbalanced him, but his
madness centered around his determination that his brother
should have neither the title nor the family fortune. As he
grew older, he grew more and more strange, and . . .
Now, remember, I had this from a maid who was sent up
from Bowwood to help in the nursery when I was a child.

What with Gervase and I and Lissa's papa, there were three of us to occupy several people, and she used to tell us stories to keep us quiet. In any case . . . now, where was I?"

Max, obviously amused, cued her. "Mad Jack didn't want his brother to inherit."

"Oh, yes. He was so determined to keep the money from his brother and nephew, for he knew he could not keep them from the title short of living forever, that he buried, over a period of years, very large sums."

"Oh, Aunt," Lissa said, rising from her Louis Quinze chair. "If this old tale were true, surely some of the treasure would have turned up."

"I think Max has a right to hear this story," Aggie said stoutly.

"But you must also tell him the tale is highly unlikely. Every great house and family has like tales of ghosts and hidden treasure. It's all a hum."

"No, no," Max insisted. "Pray, go on. This is delightful."

"Well, it's hardly fun to tell a story when everyone keeps interrupting."

"We won't interrupt," Max promised, his pointed glance for Lissa.

Since it was clear he understood that the story was just so much fustian, she sat back on her chair to finish her hot chocolate. Behind her Boysen shifted uncomfortably.

"Now, where was I?" Aggie said, her hand to her sagging coif.

"Over a period of years, Mad Jack Westmane buried large sums of money," Max said.

"Yes, you see, he turned everyone off his property. He rattled around Bowwood on his own, with only a single and equally addle-pated attendant to help him in his designs.

When one thinks of Bowwood, one can easily imagine his crazy doings. It's quite the most gothic place."

"Now, Auntie," Lissa said. "You've only been to Bowwood once, and that was when you were a girl. And that was also *after* you'd heard this tale from your nursery-maid."

"Still and all . . . And besides, Lissa, you aren't supposed to interrupt."

"I'm sorry. Pray, accept my apology."

"I do," Aggie said, poking at her hair. "Well, as I told you, Mad Jack would go out each day, maybe three or four times a day at the height of his madness. He'd dig small but very deep holes, and then drop in a few coins. He'd had everything he could converted into five-guinea pieces. They were minted in 1753 with George the Second's profile. The nurserymaid was most clear on that. He buried his whole treasure that way, all over the slopes surrounding the house. Following that, he had a rotunda built outside the library. It's situated so he could take out a chair and view the lawns. He could sit, as the nurserymaid said—sit and gloat. He felt sure that no one would ever uncover many, if any, of his five-guinea pieces, and no one ever has. Not a single one."

"Old Mad Jack was either mad or a genius," Max admitted, smiling.

"And that's not all," Aggie added. "Inside the rotunda, in gilded letters that were quite faded even when I was a little girl, he placed a riddle. One can only read it by walking the full circle of the rotunda. In fact, Mad Jack was so delighted with the taradiddle he left behind, that it's repeated twice so as to make a long line. It reads, *'Tis here, 'tis there, 'tis everywhere. Thither and yon, thither and yon.* And then, it starts again so as to run into the last. Now, if anything sounds as if he were gloating, even from his grave, it's surely that."

" 'Tis a grand tale, Aggie," Max said. "And grandly told."

" 'Tis a tale that could set you to rights if it were true," she said primly.

"Hardly. How could one ever dig up the hills around Bowwood? People would soon be calling me the maddest Westmane of all."

"Still, I wish we could give it a try," Aggie said, the light of adventure springing into her eyes. "Even if we had to retire to Bowwood, it would be worth it. Then you wouldn't be forced to go through with this marriage, with this embarrassing season."

Lissa could see that Aggie had also come around to sympathizing with Max. But Max was having none of that. Getting up, he dropped a kiss on Aggie's brow. "Here now, my dear. If I can sell out of the cavalry, especially at a time when every man-Jack of us is needed, I can certainly face a sober parson and a bride. Now," he said, moving on to the door of the little gilt and cream breakfast parlor, "I wish you all a happy day in the countryside."

In truth, Lissa had forgotten about Boysen, and the proposed jaunt. Poor man. He continued to stand behind her, patiently waiting on her decision. If only because of his patience, Lissa accepted. He went off happily to find some friends to go along.

ℰ Chapter Five

THE DRIVE to Havering pleased Lissa more than she expected, and she returned early enough to have ample time to prepare for Lord and Lady Melwick's ball. This appearance was to be Lissa's first in evening society since she'd gone into mourning—her first since the scandal. Naturally, she faced the proposition with some trepidation. Aggie, however, seemed unconcerned, and as the evening wore on, Lissa understood why.

While the Westmanes had clearly been the center of a goodly bit of gossip, their courage in putting on a brave face went far with the *beau monde*. And then, no real blame could be placed at their door. Minds and tongues had turned to what would happen next. That no one, aside from Lissa and Max, knew of the disaster which privately faced her and her aunt comforted Lissa. At some point, when she'd decided what they would do, they could quietly disappear and it would all be over.

That evening at the Melwicks', the question became not *what* the new duke would do to set things right, but *to whom* he would direct his attentions. The dowagers and duennas, the ladies who collected in little conclaves—the ones who were expert in such matters—weren't reluctant to voice their suggestions.

Only one incident marred the evening. Lord Melwick, a prosy little man of ancient bloodlines, coaxed Boysen and Lissa into his prized tobacco room which wasn't much larger than a water closet.

It was well known that tobaccos, and particularly snuff, were his lordship's especial love. If Lissa had been quicker she would have thought of a graceful refusal. Instead forty minutes later she and Boysen were still a captive audience in Lord Melwick's tobacco room.

While Boysen didn't much care for Melwick, he had a staunch respect for position and title. And Lord Melwick's lineage could be traced back to the Conquest. After the lecture was well underway, Boysen was talked into sampling Melwick's latest experiment in blended snuffs, and with the expected result. Poor Boysen began to wheeze and sneeze. Lissa was torn between feeling sorry for him and snapping at him. He'd always been susceptible to colds and coughs and aggravations of that sort, so trying snuff was foolhardy.

An hour later, watery-eyed and red-nosed, Lord Palmer finally made his excuses to his hostess. And since he'd escorted Aggie and Lissa to the ball, they left with him. Oddly enough, Lissa found their leave-taking a welcome relief. While she'd participated in society with as much liking as anyone else regularly involved, she was relieved to climb into Boysen's fine equipage and be driven home. Since this had been her first occasion out in well over a year, she also realized she could hardly be tired of company.

Unwilling to think about the cause of her boredom, she bid Boysen good night. Wishing him a quick recovery, she followed her aunt abovestairs. Aggie, too, was glad to be home and said so.

Congratulating one another on an evening that had gone well, considering the possibilities, the intimates bid their good nights. Lissa entered her bedchamber where a perfunctory Stowe awaited her return. The efficient dresser had her into her night things in a thrice. And then, Lissa was left—her frilly nightcap on her head, her hair in a thick braid, her bed turned down—to face the night. Tired as she was, relieved as she was, she was also restless. Since Pinkerton had told them that His Grace was already abed, she felt free to visit the library. The book she'd meant to fetch last night had yet to be chosen.

With a pat to Puck's silky head, Lissa went on her way. The quiet house and her solitude in the great library encouraged her to dawdle, to remember the times and books she'd shared with Aggie. Lissa smiled, her fingers tracing the spines of *The Arabian Nights*, Mr. Defoe's *Robinson Crusoe*, and *The Book of Frogs and Lilypads*. Feeling nostalgic, she chose Malory's *Morte d'Arthur*.

Passing the bronze gladiator in the entry, Lissa was back up the stairs and about to turn down the corridor in the direction of her room when she glanced to the opposite end. Max's bedchamber was a great distance from hers and Aggie's, and—

She thought her eyes deceived her. What with the flicker of her own candle and the light showing from the crack beneath his door, she thought she saw smoke. Then, she definitely smelled it. Lifting the skirts of her nightgown and wrapper, she rushed along the hall. Without a second thought—she didn't even knock—she rushed into the enormous ducal bedchamber at Westmane House.

Large, scrolled and shell-strewn Kentian furniture filled the space, but Lissa focused on the bed that dominated the rest. Within its tented recesses, Max dozed in the light of a branch of candles. He lay atop the heavily-worked counterpane, draped in a voluminous nightshirt, his feet bare, a

cigar smoldering in the second feather pillow, next to where
his head sagged.

A sudden, overwhelming fear gripped her.

"Max!" Lissa shouted.

Picking up the pillow, together with its cigar, she flew to
a bathtub of cold water that still sat on the hearth. The
smoke, billowing up from the pillow as she doused it, stung
her throat and eyes. Coughing, she fell into Max's embrace.

"Fiend seize me!" he said, awkwardly patting her back.
"I was dreaming of an encampment in Spain. I thought I
was smelling woodsmoke from an open campfire."

"I can't believe you smoke in bed," she snapped.

"I assure you, I won't anymore."

Racked with coughs, she eyed him with disgust. "Shades
of Alvanley," she gasped. "We could've all gone up in
flames."

But Max was moving to a window, flinging it wide.
"Who's Alvanley?"

"Remind me to tell you . . . when I can talk."

He was back at her side, drying her hands and forearms
with his large nightshirt. He swept up a blanket from the
bed, which he wrapped around her shoulders. Then he
pulled a robe out of the wardrobe for himself. The night air
coming in the window felt chill, and Lissa shivered. Max
calmly picked up her candlestick from where it lay snuffed
out by the richly-colored carpet, and set it, along with her
book, on his nightstand.

"Deuced brave of you, my girl. I both apologize and
thank you. I haven't seen a man act with more courage."

As she grew warmer, Lissa's anger faded. Her next
thoughts focused on housekeeping. "Why is the tub of
water still standing here?"

"Now, don't get in a pelter. I wanted to soak until the

water grew cold. By the time it did, Bagley had gone for the night, and I saw no reason to disturb the servants."

"You should have rung in any case."

"I'm not yet accustomed to being particular, my dear."

His smile tugged at her. She softened her temper. "Well, you must ring for someone now. You can't sleep in here. It smells ghastly." She moved to leave, for it was the height of impropriety to be found in the ducal bedchamber. Max caught her arm.

"It would be foolish to awaken anyone. Can't I rack up somewhere else? In a house this size, there's bound to be another bed."

His teasing grin warmed her further. She relented. How could anyone stand proof against his rough charm, she wondered. "Have you seen the duchess's bedchamber?" she asked, going to the connecting door.

"Although I'm well acquainted with the walls of the library, I haven't seen much of the rest of the house yet. How was the Melwick ball?" he asked, stopping her in her place.

"How did you know we attended the Melwick ball?"

"Aggie."

"Ah, yes. I keep forgetting you and Aggie have become bosom bows."

He shrugged a broad shoulder beneath his brocaded dressing gown. "I can't help liking her."

Lissa's best smile was wry. "That's because you're two of a kind. You're both too natural for this artificial world of ours."

Max brought the candlebranch from his bedside and they both stepped into the duchess's bedchamber. Here, everything Kentian had been swept away. The walls had white panels with delicately carved and gilded swags of fruit and flowers. A scattering of small tables and chairs, and an inlaid escritoire, were once again dominated by the bed.

Indeed, Max stood staring at the bed. "Good gad," he said. "A less likely contraption for sleeping, I've yet to see."

The bed was carved and gilded in flowers, seeded fruits, and cherubs. The chubby fellows flew about it in happy abandon. They clung to its bedposts, supported its draperies, and beckoned from its headboard. One pair at the very top flirted in an embrace from which fell the yards and yards of rose silk that formed the tented roof and then swagged into draperies.

"A former duchess brought it back from Venice," she said.

"Leave it to the Venetians. Decadent. Down to a man," he murmured. "But with the right person, I could ask a small fortune for it."

"Sell it?" she exclaimed, until she saw the light in his amber eyes. She realized she had to learn to fall in with his sense of humor. Exactly when she'd become so starchy, she couldn't imagine. Aggie hadn't raised her to be starchy.

"And who is this 'right person' who'd be interested in giving you a fortune for the bed?" she asked lightly.

He paused to peer at her, the light from his golden branch of candles flickering over his craggy features. "I see, now, the mistake I've made. I must learn to guard my tongue."

Lissa's wry smile tugged at her lips. "You've set yourself a difficult task. But who is the 'right person' to pay a fortune for the bed?"

"I shouldn't have said that. Pray, forget it."

Squaring her small frame, Lissa faced his large, robe-clad figure. "Who? Tell me."

"Ladies don't know the sort of female who'd pay for such a bed."

Despite herself, Lissa blushed.

"I was only funning, Damalis," he said gently. "I won't sell the bed. Not unless everything else must be sold."

Opening a small cupboard concealed in the paneling, Lissa loaded her arms with fresh linens. She dumped her burden on a chair, then went to remove the counterpane that was embroidered with courting unicorns.

She took pride in the house; she knew she managed it well. She had no fears that the revealed mattress hadn't been recently aired. Nor would there be so much as a speck of dust on even the uppermost cherub.

"This will go much more quickly and easily if you'll move to the other side and help me, Your Grace."

Although it was evident that His Grace didn't know what she expected of him, he was immediately willing. When Lissa shook out the sheet over the mattress, he followed her lead, tucking it in as he should.

"The lavender smells wonderful," he said. "When we were on the road, Bagley and I, we invariably looked for lavender in the windows at inns. Lavender displayed like that was a fairly reliable sign of good housekeeping."

"I can imagine the places you might have fallen victim to."

He grinned. "No, my dear. You cannot imagine."

Going back to her pile, Lissa carefully laid aside the next spray of lavender, and took the subsequent sheet. "Just because, Your Grace, we have led different lives, doesn't mean you can laud it over me at every turn."

"Ha! And look who's saying I laud it over you? What about our meeting in the entry that first day? Um? Who was it that stuck her sweet little nose in the air, claiming the looks and coloring of a Westmane and suggesting I didn't come close?"

Once again, Lissa blushed. Still, she kept her hands busy

with the pillowcases. "I . . . I'm sorry," she said, her eyes lowered to a case she jerked around a pillow. "I—"

"Say no more," Max said with his usual generosity. "I thought you were quite adorably feminine. I was telling the truth when I said I'd never had a homecoming. You see, I've never really had a home."

"But what about your father in Oxford?"

"Except for the advanced lessons he gave me, I hardly saw him. And our shared rooms were anything but a home. My mama died in giving birth and my father was already an elderly gentleman with no use for noisy brats. While I was good at my studies, I didn't want to stay on and step into his shoes. I like to think I could have become good enough to have done so, but I wanted adventure."

Lissa and Max tucked in the final blanket. She didn't know what to say. She also knew he didn't expect sympathy—he had simply recounted his past. "I noticed in the library," she ventured, "that you continue to translate."

He'd gone to light a fire, and he didn't look at her when he spoke. "When I'm worried, or at my wit's end, I work at translating phrases. Honing and rehoning them. It sounds strange, but translating soothes me. My fellow officers used to roast me about it, but I always had my book with me. When I had a moment, I'd pull it out and . . . well . . ."

They'd finished, and he stood before the blazing fire. Lissa had never before seen a man in the state of undress. He looked wonderful. His large feet remained bare, just visible beneath his full-length dressing gown. His big hands hung unusually quiet at his sides. The room was ready and welcoming, redolent with the scent of lavender, and she moved to leave.

"That reminds me," he said, passing her as they reentered the now chill but still badly smelling ducal bedchamber. "Come. You must look at this."

Lissa accepted his copy of the Greek play, the one she'd seen on his desk in the library.

"Open it to the frontispiece," he urged.

She peered at him, puzzled. Still, she opened the worn, calf-bound volume. He stood above her, hovering at her shoulder. This little book, which had followed him as he'd traced out his difficult life, looked every inch as if it had always been in his pocket.

"There," he said. "Stamped directly into the paper. See the little head? I was thinking, tonight, when I was studying her again, that she resembles you. I first noticed it when I saw you in the entry. But now, I'm sure of it. Oh, I realize the tight cap of curls isn't at all similar to your glorious red mane. But look at that straight little nose, those widely set eyes, that pouty underlip. She's you to a mote. Strange, isn't it?" he said. "I've been carrying your likeness about with me for years."

Once again, Lissa didn't know what to say. He leaned so near to her. She sensed the vitality of his large body. She thought about their states of undress. They could have been lovers.

"The best part, of course, is your name," he said.

She could feel the heat in her cheeks. "My name?" His thoughts were so ordinary. And hers were not.

"Yes. Damalis. It translates from the Greek as 'the conqueror.' "

"It does?"

"You mean, you didn't know?"

"No. Never. I was named for a great aunt."

"That may be, but the result is the same. You have a name that suits you down to the ground. You're a brave little soldier. You saved my life tonight."

Lissa tried to sound light. "Dumping a smoldering feather pillow into a cold bath is hardly an act of bravery."

"Anytime anyone does something they're afraid to do, my dear Damalis, it's an act of courage. Surely, you felt afraid. And that's the definition of bravery. To go ahead and do what you're afraid to do."

Looking into Max's face with its faint scar, Lissa knew he was the expert in this instance. She wondered how many times, how many hours in any given day, he'd done something, all the while his brave heart had thudded in his broad chest.

"I'd better go," she said, undraping the blanket she wore from around her shoulders.

But he pressed nearer, his golden eyes honeyed. "How about a thank you kiss?"

Lissa stiffened. "You've thanked me already."

When she turned away, he grasped her arm, his eyes dancing with delight. "You kissed me in the library."

"It was *you* who kissed *me* in the library."

"It was very nice, *cousin*. Oh, yes, I heard how you introduced me to Lord Palmer as *cousin*. Baggage," he drawled.

"You are too free, sir. It will never do."

"Point taken, my dear." Letting go of her arm, he moved to the nighttable to fetch the candle and book she'd dropped on coming in. "But I warn you, I shall never be a lap dog."

Nor did she want him to be. But she didn't say that.

"And, that reminds me. Lord Palmer will be here in the morning to help with my cravats."

"Are you implying that Boysen *is* a lap dog?"

"Never, my dear," he said, grinning. "I never imply when I can speak plainly. And with you, I speak my mind. We are friends, remember?"

ℰ Chapter Six

WHEN PUCK STRETCHED and yawned at the foot of her bed, Lissa woke up. She realized she'd finally slept long and hard. The watery sunlight that had awakened the Pekingese indicated the day was far advanced, and she swung out of bed with a neat movement. "You must need to go out," she said to the dog.

He perked his ears and wagged his tail. After ten years of companionship, he understood the basics of their routines, especially those involving himself. Lissa knew she'd spoiled him. He never paid her weak attempts at controlling him any heed. And no one, including Aggie, liked him.

But somehow, Lissa couldn't reprimand the dog. He'd been a part of her past. A great comfort when her fiancé had died.

Vernon had been vital. Young. Like she, not much above seventeen. Lissa had met him at an early age in Oxfordshire. He'd been the son of a neighboring house, and they'd become immediate and boon companions. Every summer and any holiday she could, Lissa had gone to Oxfordshire, and the adults involved had looked on with a tolerant approval.

A life with Vernon, settled in the country, had seemed all Lissa could hope for. And then, it had been over—in not much above the wink of an eye.

Lissa had returned to London. She'd taken an amazing hold on herself. She'd managed her come-out season with a notable aplomb for one of her tender years. Even more amazingly, the following season had marked her first as her uncle's hostess. By that time she also held the reins at Westmane House, and everyone, including herself, had thought she'd recovered from her loss.

She, however, had begun to wonder. Had she merely disciplined herself as she had not Puck? Hadn't she grown steadily starchier with every passing year? And was starchiness, a strict adherence to society's every expectation, simply a way of carrying on?

She tugged at the bell rope, endeavoring to put those bothersome thoughts aside. A footman came for Puck, a maid delivered her hot chocolate and saw to her fire, while Stowe began the routine of bath and personal preparations. Still, Lissa knew this would not be another ordinary morning. Boysen Palmer would be here soon to show Max how to properly tie a cravat.

Hadn't Max reminded her of that just last night—while in his nightclothes, in his bedchamber? Well, that experience she would also endeavor to put from her mind.

Finally dressed in a morning gown of jonquil cambric with two rows of worked trimming at the hem, Lissa could no longer remain in her bedchamber. Nor would she find Aggie in the breakfast parlor. It was too late in the morning, and Aggie had said something about paying a call on an ailing Mrs. Maypost, her very best friend. Curious, but not wanting to indulge her curiosity, Lissa let herself out into the second-floor corridor, Puck following.

The house was quiet. Could she have slept through Boysen's visit?

Then she saw Max's batman. He balanced a tray of glasses and decanter of wine as he entered the duke's room.

As usual, Puck began to growl and hop about, merely upon seeing Bagley. Now, despite Lissa's attempt to stop him, he tracked the fellow. What with his hands being occupied with the tray, Bagley had a hard enough task in opening the bedchamber door. And then, barking wildly, Puck rushed passed the batman into the male sanctum.

Lissa winced. She could hear the immediate commotion. Puck barked, Bagley apologized to his colonel, while Boysen spoke to his valet.

"Don't worry, Pinseat," she heard Lord Palmer say. "Never fear. I'll . . . kerchoo . . . catch him."

Still, Lissa stood outside the cracked door, every sound from within drawing a picture of what followed. Puck continued to carry on, while Boysen continued to reassure his man. Ensuing thumps and bumps indicated the usual fruitless attempts at catching the little beast. The aggravating game Lissa so often played was on again.

Several moments passed, but to no avail. If anything, the hubbub increased. Lissa's cheeks grew hotter. She was entirely to blame. She wondered how Max had reacted. Thoughts of his certain enjoyment of this humiliating scene caused a flood of ire to bubble up inside of her. Before she knew it, she'd swung wide the door and stepped into the room.

The chamber of the night before had disappeared. No bath sat at the hearth. No smoke hung like a pall. Dim sunlight exposed a pristine room with four gentlemen brought up short with surprise.

"Why, Lissa my dear," Boysen said, the most surprised of all.

"I'm sorry about Puck," she apologized. "I thought I might be of help."

Max's eyes mocked her. He stood as she could have expected, his arms akimbo, fully-dressed, a neatly tied cravat puffing from his waistcoat just as it should. He was thoroughly enjoying, if not the occasion, then what the occasion had become.

"Good morning, Your Grace," she said, straightening her shoulders.

"Cousin," he said, with an infuriating grin.

Puck had run a stickish figure to ground—one who could only be Pinseat. The man was perched on a chair, his long legs beneath him, a fresh cravat draping over the shoulder of his perfectly cut black-cloth coat.

Oh, yes. Max was in alt. And *she* was not supposed to be there.

"Pray, dear Lissa," Boysen said, torn between rescuing his valet and his shock at her stubborn stance. "You must wait in the hall. I'll catch the dog and bring him out to you."

"Now, now," Max said, all affability. "That doesn't sound very courteous of us, Palmer old fellow."

While the dog continued to yap, Boysen made himself heard over the noise. "It isn't a question of courtesy, Your Grace. Lissa should not be in here."

Max's gaze danced to hers. "Oh, but she's been here before."

For all his teasing, Lissa couldn't believe Max would betray her so thoroughly. Giving him a fulminating look, she gathered her dignity about her and stood her ground.

But he was continuing, ignoring the look of shock in Boysen's pale eyes. "She sat with her uncle, you know. In his last days," he added, as if recalling an admirable duty well done.

Boysen was properly appreciative. "Oh, I see."

Of course, Lissa had never done any such duty. Her uncle had no more wished for her presence in his last hours than he'd had any personal use for her before those hours. But Max was teasing them all.

"I'd like very much for my cousin to stay for a moment," he said to Boysen. "I want her to see this marvel that Pinseat is able to perform with no more than a strip of cloth. That's enough, old fellow," Max directed at the dog. Puck went stock still. Once again, a final yap marked his immediate capitulation, and he flew out of the room as quickly as he'd come in.

"Now, cousin," Max said to Lissa, "you must have a chair."

"But . . . but . . ." While Pinseat cautiously undid his long legs and climbed down from his own heavily carved and gilded bastion, Boysen floundered. "Truly, Your Grace. Lissa cannot remain."

"Just for a moment," Max said. "It won't hurt. No one here will tell. And besides, she's my *cousin*."

While it was clear that Boysen did not agree, he deferred to Max. Max was, after all, a duke.

Lissa sank onto the chair Bagley fetched and the farce went on with an audience of one.

"How do you like this knot, Cousin? What is it called again, Pinseat?"

The stickish man had regained his composure, and in a manner which reflected his master's station, replied, " 'Tis called the Waterfall, Your Grace."

Bagley, Lissa noticed, appeared more disgruntled than ever. Still, he stood, looking as if he should pay attention, his thoughts evident as they tracked across his crude features.

"Ah, yes. The Waterfall." Max's eyes glowed, but only for Lissa. "We began with a haircut. A *coup du vent*, I believe. We've since tied our way through the Oriental, the Mathematical, and the Waterfall, with a few of Lord Petersham's favorites thrown in for good measure. We're thinking we'll leave the *Trone d'amour* for another day, when my fingers are more adept at such intricacies."

Lissa felt about to explode. But Boysen, in all seriousness, distracted her. "Actually, Lissa dear, I think you must excuse us now."

"But why?" Max insisted. "Damalis has offered to assist me in my efforts to improve myself. She can hardly be compromised at witnessing my progress in tying knots."

"But," Boysen insisted, in his turn, "that is not the point, Your Grace. That she be present in your bedchamber is simply not the thing."

"Damalis is my tutor," Max said, all innocence. "To please you, I will turn my back when I'm without a cravat. Please, you must let her see Pinseat work his magic."

Pinseat allowed a pleased smile. Boysen reluctantly conceded. Bagley rolled his eyes in a blatant disbelief that any of this could be happening. Max continued his farcical act. Lissa was bid to attend carefully while Pinseat's bony fingers tied seven more perfect Waterfalls, one after the other.

In the end Boysen came around enough to describe the Palmer Frond. He and his gentleman's gentleman had perfected his own invention no more recently than last month. They hoped to spring the knot on the *ton* at the height of the season. The neckcloth itself had to be prepared in advance. Tiny pleats were—as was explained in alternating speeches between master and man—painstakingly pressed into the highly starched strip. After the knot was completed—Pinseat chimed with a flush of pride—the ends fell into small fans. Those, Max himself had suggested, should be called "fronds," or so Boysen claimed.

"You see, it suits the name of Palmer," Boysen explained unnecessarily. "Truly, His Grace is most kind in taking an interest," he added, pleasure like a pink flush in his cheeks.

Max's eyes twinkled. But Lissa had had enough. Rising from her chair, she thanked them for demonstrating their expertise. As she went down the hall she felt her irritation roil around inside her. Max's mockery of Boysen's ridiculous behavior had her equally frustrated with both men. She was glad to escape them.

Early that evening, Lissa sat in the painted parlor waiting for her aunt. Lord Palmer was to act as their escort, this time to a musicale.

When Max stuck his head in at the door, he interrupted her thoughts. "Are you still angry with me?" he asked.

"It's no concern of mine if you play the buffoon."

"Come now, Damalis. Don't turn Miss Prunes and Prisms on me. I could hardly take such folderol seriously, now could I?"

With an effort to overcome her stickiest behavior—to fulfill her decision to rise above it—Lissa peered at her tormentor. "I suppose not," she agreed, albeit reluctantly. Still, Max's resultant smile beguiled her. "Your efforts," she added dryly, "didn't improve your cravat-tying skills, I see."

"No, this one's quite a mess. I have these large fingers, and . . . well, Bagley's dug in his heels and refuses to learn altogether. I brought a few fresh cravats along in hopes that you—"

"But this isn't at all proper." Even if she weren't to behave like Miss Prunes and Prisms, Lissa knew she was just as sticky as Boysen had been that morning.

"I simply don't understand why not," Max said with some exasperation. "What harm did it do for you to be in my bedchamber this morning? In fact, we must admit that last night it did a great deal of good."

"You have to look at it differently or it will cause some

real harm. Servants gossip, and gossip gets out of hand no
matter how . . . well, I might as well step out into
Piccadilly and tie my garters as to tie your cravat and have
someone find out."

"Tie your garters on in Piccadilly, eh?" he asked, with a
grin.

Clearly she shouldn't have encouraged him.

"On the other hand," he added, "it's just as well you
don't. I'd feel obliged to knock down anyone who observed. A cousinly duty, you understand."

"Never mind . . . but, yes," she said on an exaggerated sigh. "I'll tie your cravat, if only to get rid of you."

"Just to show how grateful I am, I'll promise never to
make sport of Boysen again. He was kind in offering his
help, and I'd even apologize to him for this morning, if he
knew I'd offended him."

"I think we'd better drop this subject before I use this
cravat as a noose," she said dryly.

The pair moved to a window, the last light of day
breaking through the clouds to shine on them. As Max went
docile under her fingers, Lissa felt as if she'd somehow
captured some powerful and yet free spirit. His breath
tugged at her curls and wafted over her cheeks. The clean
scent of his starched linens filled her senses. She could
scarcely keep her mind to her task. Her first two tries at
Max's requested Waterfall were adequate, but the third was
as perfect as any she'd seen Pinseat turn out.

"Ha!" Max exclaimed when he went to view her endeavor in a glass. "It's too bad I can't flaunt this under
Pinseat's long nose. It's every bit as good as any he tied.
We should contrive a new knot together. Something as
elaborate as the devil's own handiwork. We could spring it
on The Fashionables a day after the Palmer Frond makes its
debut. We'd quite cast them in the shade." Catching Lissa's

stern expression next to his own reflection in the glass, he smiled more softly. "No more, no more, I promise. I can't afford to offend my only ally."

"I suppose Aunt Aggie has told you she's discovered the date of Daphne Huntley's come-out ball?"

"Yes, I put it down. She says she's sure to get us invitation cards."

"And two nights hence? Do you have plans?"

"I'm at your beck and call."

"You must come out into mixed society. It would be good to attend the opera. Aside from Almack's, the opera is the place to be seen."

He smiled. "You mean, if I attend the opera, the *ton* will be less likely to think me some uncouth fellow who doesn't deserve the title."

"I'm saying that if you attend the opera everyone will be watching. Besides, it's fustian to think anyone will find you uncouth."

"Ah, but you found me so, at first. Or rather, you thought you'd find me so."

Damalis was too honest to evade this. "I fully admit I believed you would never do as Westmane. I thought that if you couldn't be Westmane in the style of my uncle and those before him, that you wouldn't suit at all. I've come to see, however, that while you are indeed not cut from the same bolt, you're equally as suitable. In many ways, you already surpass your predecessors. In the short time you've been here, you've shown more concern for the duchy than my uncle did in his whole life," she ended primly.

Max grinned. She'd won that skirmish. "Spoken as honestly as I would've expected. No dissembler, is my Damalis."

The admiration and warmth in Max's eyes—although pleasing to Lissa—pushed her toward another subject. "I think we should spend some time on your speech. You're far too blunt. It will never do. Social conversation is a game played with finesse. It's meant to impress. You'll be judged by it more than you can imagine. Why don't we begin day after tomorrow, following breakfast?"

"By Jove. Small talk in the morning and the opera at night. I may not get up from my bed."

With his most exaggerated masculine sigh, Max said, "I shall have to think of something special as payment for all the good you do me. In the meanwhile, I wish you a happy evening."

Lissa was on the verge of telling him about the strict societal rules against his giving her gifts, but she thought he'd had enough for now. In any case, she certainly had.

✍ Chapter Seven

THE ROYAL OPERA HOUSE acted as both rival and companion piece to Drury Lane Theatre. Within its walls beat the very heart of London society. Here the patronesses of Almack's not only watched over those who were allowed to buy tickets, but by default, took the place of royalty. Here the beauties came to show off their beauty, the wealthy to display their wealth. Here, Brummell and his coterie sat in Fop's Alley so as to have their say. Little on stage compared to the performance given by the audience.

In urging Max to attend, Lissa knew what they were braving. She also knew he wouldn't get far in society—even at its private balls and card parties—if he didn't nod to the patronesses first. And so, she coaxed him to attend. She was no longer worried about the appearance he'd make. She'd decided, as the days went along and he gained more experience with fashion, that he didn't look merely well in standard gentlemen's attire; he was a confident male who could draw every attention. And for now that would be enough. Aside from any major gaffe, which she trusted he had the good sense to avoid, she expected all to go well.

Still, she did wonder.

She stood in the upper corridor of the theater, outside the private boxes. Those who mattered collected in dazzling

groups, indulging in light exchanges. She herself listened
with half an ear to Aggie, Boysen, and some friends. But
she also kept an eye on Max's progress through the crowd.
While it was obvious, by the frequent introductions, that he
remained unfamiliar with most of the ladies, he was handed
along from one gentleman to the next with either a smile or
even a clap on the back. He was clearly well liked. Indeed,
he was doing well. With the men.

Lissa was now concerned about how he would fare with
the ladies. Especially Daphine Huntley. When he bowed
over a lady's hand, he didn't use the formal yet light address
expected. He simply moved through the crowd, friendly but
not essentially courtly—not out to please. They'd have to
work on him before the come-out ball.

She and her aunt had tried to teach him proper protocol
that morning, directly after breakfast. He'd relaxed on his
chair, stretching out his long legs, while he'd listened to
both Lissa's instructions and Aggie's occasional comments.
Lissa had drawn up whole lists, regarding everything from
priorities in introductions to seating arrangements at table.
Max's position as a duke entitled him to more consider-
ations than most, and she felt it important that he learn both
what would be accorded to him as well as what would be
expected of him. The subjects had been complicated and
boring, and Lissa had feared overwhelming him with too
much at once.

After listening silently for some time, he'd parroted back
enough to her, almost verbatim, so as to demonstrate he'd
not only been attending but that he'd understood.

When she'd told him that his ability to pick up such
complicated matters easily amazed her, he'd given her his
most charming smile. "You forget, my dear, I spent many
years in a service whose pecking order and protocol are, if
anything, more important."

Yet, to Lissa's mind, he needed to understand a fine distinction she didn't know how to put across to him. Perhaps, experience would be his best teacher. While eccentricity, even some deviation, was acceptable among The Exclusives, it wouldn't do in Max's case—not until his personal position had been secured. And no debutante would favor a man who wasn't accepted.

Tonight, Max ended up fairly near to Lissa, in an exchange with Lady Shellcross. The marchioness was an impressive matron, the sort of woman Lissa would have sought out if their paths had crossed more often. Her ladyship was both intelligent and respected.

Inching closer to Max and his companion, Lissa could hear that the conversation centered on opera. Of course, some mention of travel had to be included, because their experiences encompassed any number of performances in other cities—cities far better known for their music than London. They spoke of Neapolitan *opera seria*. Because it usually presented a conflict of human passions, based on some story from an ancient Greek or Latin author, Max admitted to a penchant for such evenings. *Opera buffa* caused a shared chuckle. Totally engrossed, the pair agreed that tonight's lighter fare of English ballad opera was typical of the English.

A fire kindled in Lissa.

It wasn't quite jealousy, although she did wish she could have had a part in the exchange. Her anger was instead focused on Max. She saw that he'd made sport of her, just as he had Boysen. Thinking back, she recalled her brief explanation of tonight's libretto—an explanation she'd made in hopes of preparing Max so he'd better enjoy himself. "Thank you," he had said, smiling.

Had that smile been softly mocking? She hadn't thought so at the time, but clearly it had been. After all, Max had mocked Boysen even more openly, and Boysen hadn't caught on.

Anger rose like bile in Lissa's throat.

Then she remembered other instances. Max had smiled at her, just so, that very morning. She'd warned him against the possible entrapment in seeking a breath of fresh air with a lady on a secluded terrace. Or, in dancing with the same partner more than twice in an evening. He'd laughed openly, then. Even when he must have seen she'd been as serious as a stick. How could he? How dare he, when she'd been trying to help?

A flush spread into Lissa's face. She could feel it. When she looked up at him, he was watching her with his smiling, amber gaze. There! She could see it plainly. He was sending her that secretive smile—that cat's grin which said he'd caught her eavesdropping like some ill-mannered chit. He found her amusing. Lifting her straight, patrician nose, Lissa stared haughtily at him before turning her back completely.

Later, when he offered himself as escort to their box, she turned to Boysen instead. She would never have done that by choice.

As Lissa sat in her bed that night, Max simply stalked into her room, slamming her door behind him. Puck's little body jerked with surprise.

"What . . . what are you doing here?" Lissa said, gasping with disbelief.

"I've come to ask why you cut me at the opera."

"I don't care to discuss it. And I certainly don't want the whole household to know of this unheard of impropriety on your part. This is too much, even for you!"

"I won't leave, even if the whole neighborhood hears of it."

"And I thought you a gentleman."

"And I thought you my friend."

The pair stared at each other. Except for his loosened cravat, Max remained fully clothed. He looked more appealing than ever, even as his angry gaze bored into hers. The firelight caught in his eyes, turning them to the deepest honey.

"One does not laugh at a friend."

"Good gad! Whatever gave you the caper-witted notion that I laugh at you? You're the only one in this whole rotten mess I can laugh *with*." Max's inflection revealed how hurt he'd been. "Bagley, my lifelong companion and the only one I have left of my past, feels out of place here. He's defected to his own ranks. As much as I like Aggie, as much as I know she cares for me, I'd hardly call her a confidant. If I so much as drop a hint that I have no wish to be Westmane, my friends think me mad. Since my arrival in London, all I've had for any sense of sanity has been you. And now, for what reason I cannot imagine, you turn up your little nose and cut me dead."

"You caught me eavesdropping on your conversation with the marchioness! It was quite clear that you know more about opera than I ever will. You sent me one of your wicked smiles to put me in my place."

He smiled ruefully. "Clearly, I'm unaccustomed to softer, female company. Sometimes you amaze me." Max turned away. He paced toward the fire, where he went on more conversationally. "I apologize. Not for the smile. I have nothing to apologize for in that. I do realize, however, that I tend to act unconventionally with you. And for that, I beg your pardon. In this particular case, tonight at the opera . . . well, you would like Lady Shellcross and I was on the verge of suggesting an introduction. You obviously misread my signal. Friends?"

"Then, you weren't laughing at me this morning? And what about the other times I've suspected it? Your laughing at Boysen doesn't recommend you, you know."

"I've never laughed at you. If anything, I've endeavored to tell you how much I appreciate your help. I've obviously made a mull of things."

Max stood next to the fire. The shadows softened his masculinity. He seemed vulnerable. As it invariably did, her heart went out to him. "I also hope we can make this up," she said.

His sweet smile suited the moment. "So, we cry peace, then?"

"Peace."

"I felt horribly under fire, you know."

Lissa chuckled. "Hardly."

"Oh, no. You can be most formidable when you want to be."

"I can't imagine you being intimidated."

"You certainly don't look intimidating now," he admitted softly, averting his eyes to the fire and collecting himself so as to go on more like themselves. "I suppose it's Palmer who's to be the lucky man."

Lissa's heart thudded. "Perhaps."

"You haven't decided?"

"Not really." Lissa dared not mention the pressure she felt because of her lost funds. Max had said he'd be responsible for her and Aggie. If she told him she wanted to remove them from his accumulating burdens, he'd fly into the boughs.

"Well," he said, locking his hands behind his back and considering the ceiling. "Don't rush into anything. There's no need to rush."

"Thank you."

"And then, there are two more points," he added, even more relaxed. "Although I'm not entirely without experience, and what with Daphne Huntley's ball coming up, I thought you might . . ."

"Act as dancing master?"

He smiled. "Yes."

"A few mornings following breakfast should do. Aunt Aggie can play for us. But I warn you, she can only approximate the tunes you'll hear at the balls."

Max chuckled, then sobered for his final point. "Aggie says you handle the ribbons as well as any man."

Lissa didn't reply.

He pushed on. "I've ordered a curricle. A hired one, since I can't afford one of my own. Deuced expensive contraptions. Still, no gentleman in London seems to be without a light carriage, and while I much prefer riding . . . Well, as my courting tutor, you must admit that I can hardly throw a maid across my saddlebow. I'd hoped," he said, meeting her gaze levelly, "that you would teach me how to drive."

"I can't."

Max came toward her slowly. He sat on the edge of her bed and took her hands in his large, warm grasp. His hands seemed familiar now, as did his warmth, his unique scent of tobacco and starched linens. His voice. "Aggie told me about young Markham. She says he taught you to drive."

"And to row a boat, to bait a hook, and to shoot woodcock. But I can't teach you how to drive. I'm afraid of carriages."

"But don't you see? This is where I can help you. I think, between the pair of us, that you can drive again—that you can feel comfortable in a light carriage again. You must let me help you in this."

Denying him was hard, but Lissa shook her head.

"Promise me, you'll at least think about it," he urged.

She remained reluctant, but she wanted him to leave now. His nearness unnerved her. "I'll think about it."

"I know you can do it. You've got bottom, my girl."

Lissa allowed a little smile. But he, rather than getting up and leaving as she'd hoped, leaned closer to her, his face confronting hers with a light smile. "How about a kiss, Damalis? Middle-of-the-night kisses and meetings are traditional with us, you know."

"They're no such thing."

"You let me kiss you in the library when we sealed our wager."

"I didn't *let* you. And I don't much *like* our wager."

"I won't be a gentleman, however, and let you out of it." He studied her features for a moment. His eyes were a honeyed delight. "What do you say to a kiss to prove we've made up?"

"No. You really must say goodnight now."

His brows lifted. "A goodnight kiss, then?"

"No."

"I suppose I'll simply have to take full responsibility and kiss you for not much reason at all."

"This is horrid of you, Max."

"I said, I'll take the blame," he whispered, finally using those wonderful lips for more than teasing her, for more than smiling at her.

He was warm and gentle and tentative. He was Max, and Lissa's heart soared . . .

But then he smiled and moved to stand above her. "I'm glad we're friends again."

She watched him leave. At the door, he had the sense to crack it and peer down the hall. With a little wave, he left.

Lissa's eyes locked with Puck's pop-eyed stare. "After all these years of bluff and bluster, you would have to fail me now."

The next day she and Aggie were promised to Boysen for a carriage ride. As it turned out, Boysen's information concerning the little Norman church in East Ham proved true. Sitting in a wide churchyard with much wildlife about, it remained unspoiled since its construction in the first half of the twelfth century. A suitable tower had been added in the sixteenth, and inside, its stone interior, its blind arcade, round arches and windows, were very charming.

" 'Tis said," Boysen stated, looking at Lissa from where he'd been examining a round marble font set on a balaster pedestal, "that the inscription on the bell reads, 'I am sweet honey; I am called the bell of Gabriel.' Sounds delightful, does it not? I should like to hear it ring."

Lissa nodded, noting his pale smile and his pale pleasure. Surely she was just looking for excuses, she told herself. Still, she couldn't bring herself to say it. Not just yet. Allowing her eyes to lead her, she tracked the arch over the inner door to the nave. Traces of wall painting made her realize how truly old the edifice was. The font Boysen examined dated to 1639, the bell he spoke of, 1380.

"Seems a shame to rush," he said, "but Lady Agatha can't be comfortable waiting for us in the carriage."

"She said she wouldn't mind if we stopped. In any case, when I went to look, she was dozing."

"Even so, it's much warmer in the carriage," Boysen said, uselessly chafing the sleeves of his coat.

Although he liked traveling around the countryside, he invariably complained about the weather. Then again, it wasn't all that warm on this day in late April. And then, Lissa knew she was searching for reasons to refuse him.

Once again, her eyes drifted over the brasses, the monuments to those lives, big and small, that had gone before. So long before. St. Mary Magdalene parish church even had an altar tomb. Crammed into the northeastern side of the apse, it recalled Edmund and Jane Neville. The countess's coronet, sitting on the brow of her effigy, reached out to Lissa's heart. Because her husband had supported the effort to set Mary, Queen of Scots on the throne of England in 1569, he'd lost the title. What Jane Neville had been denied in life, she wore in death.

Truly, Lissa admonished herself inwardly. You're being ridiculous. Square your shoulders, my girl, and get on with it. But then, she almost didn't. Boysen was coming toward her to take her arm. He'd decided to leave, and she didn't have time to talk to him after all. Then she heard her own voice, sounding out in the chill, hollow spaces of the dimly lit Norman church.

"Wait, Boysen. Just a moment."

He paused, of course, his gloved hand still stretched toward her elbow. Inquiry marked his pale grey eyes.

"I . . . I think it only right that you know."

He continued to look puzzled, his hand drifting down.

"When my uncle ruined the Westmane fortune, he also ruined mine. And my aunt's. Since . . . since you are expecting an answer from me . . . a reply to your proposal of marriage, I think it only fair that I warn you . . . that I let you withdraw your offer. I am not what I was when you first proposed."

He stared at her, almost as if struck. For a moment, Lissa thought she'd misjudged his probable reaction. She'd thought Boysen, with his fortune, hadn't been considering the inheritance she would have brought as Westmane's niece. And now, she wondered—hoped—that she'd been wrong.

"Oh, Lissa. Poor Lissa," he said, moving closer. "Surely, you can't believe this news will make me withdraw. On the contrary, I insist on pushing my suit. Except for the talk that will surely arise, I don't care a fig about your lost inheritance."

Lissa didn't know whether to return his weakly warm smile or to surprise them both and weep. Still, she managed to carry on. It was her own fault for letting it go so far. "Well, then. If what you say is true, I shall be happy to accept your proposal."

He smiled gently. "Oh, Lissa, my dear. I am quite bereft of words."

"Yes . . . well, I do have one small request."

"And what is that, my dear? Anything, anything, at all."

"If we might keep our engagement a secret. Just for a little while."

And then, the question she'd expected. "But why, my dear?"

She returned her neatly prepared answer. "I think it best that we allow His Grace a little more time to adjust, a little more time to settle his own affairs. He's working assiduously to that end, you know. I still can't desert him or make it appear as if Aunt Aggie and I find anything wrong with his succeeding." She paused. "You do mean to accept Aunt Aggie into your household as well, do you not? When you first proposed, you said—"

"Oh, yes, yes. I like your aunt very well. She'll always be welcome. But as to your request for a secret engagement . . . While to some extent I can understand, I don't think you need to concern yourself with the new duke."

"But he's family, and I should like to be faithful to what very little family I have left, Boysen."

Once again he looked at her, his breath the slightest bit of fog adrift on the cool air inside the stone church. "Well, I suppose. I can't like it, but . . ."

"Oh, Boysen. You are too good."

For a moment, Lissa thought he might bend forward and press his lips to hers. But he didn't. Instead, he dropped an awkward peck on her cheek.

"Remember. We'll not tell even Aunt," she cautioned, as they headed for the door.

He nodded a reluctant little nod. "All right. But not for long, Lissa. We've waited much too long already, and I truly believe my own family has some rights in this. Especially my dear mama. She's been waiting these many years for me to marry. She quite likes you, Lissa. She, above everyone, will be beyond herself with joy."

While Lissa wanted to give Boysen his point, something in her held tenaciously to her desire for keeping their secret. Even when they climbed into the carriage to join Aggie—even when Lissa felt somewhat guilty—she easily kept her tongue between her teeth. Precisely how she would guard such a secret, and for how long, she hadn't decided. It was more that she needed time—her own time to adjust to the idea of marrying Boysen.

She knew it was right that she leave Westmane House. She did not want to be a burden to Max. Indeed, once he married, his new wife wouldn't appreciate any old maid "cousins." No, to marry Boysen was the best answer. She'd been on the verge of accepting his proposal for a long while, and now it was time to do so.

In any case, Boysen Palmer was exactly what Lissa wanted in a husband. He didn't expect her love. He was uncomfortable with that particular emotion himself. They'd rub along well. They were invariably honest with each other, and honesty would stand them in the best stead.

Perfect. It was perfect. Lissa would have the children and

the home she wanted. Aunt Aggie would be secure. Boysen would have his ideal—the wife who would run his house, act as his hostess, share his tame amusements, and by and large, leave him to his own devices. It was, indeed, the perfect solution. She would soon feel good about it, she was sure.

Chapter Eight

LADY AGATHA WESTMANE sat at the pianoforte in the
ballroom at Westmane House trying to plunk out a waltz.
Nothing about their recent mornings, spent in polishing
Max's dancing skills, was worthy of the lovely couple
revolving on the vast stretch of parqueted floor. And that
was particularly true of her accompaniment.

While the anti-Kentian duchess had softened the enormous room with Waterford glass chandeliers, those were
draped. Just as were the dozens of delicate gilt chairs that
lined the walls. Max had thrown back the curtains on
several of the large windows to let in a veritable flood of
light, but the draped pictures, the draped musicians' stands
and chairs, even the half-draped pianoforte, were revealed
for what they were. Merely mute onlookers to a charming
sight.

Aggie thought there should rather be hundreds of flickering tapers and dozens and dozens of dazzling guests.
There had been often enough in the past. To her mind, it
was just as well those days were gone. A new breeze, fresh
and strong, swept through Westmane House. And that was
just as well, too.

Aggie smiled approvingly at Lissa who was dressed in a
morning gown of pale, ruby merino cloth. She had a

delightful figure and a trim ankle, and her skirts swayed about her as they should. She smiled up into her partner's equally smiling face. Max, Aggie could hear, hummed as an endeavor to smooth the tune when Aggie's old fingers could not.

She wasn't doing them justice, but it didn't seem to bother the couple a jot. Nor did the Holland-bedraped furniture appear to matter. The three of them simply enjoyed.

Well, the four of them, actually. Puck slept on a chair. Aggie found his proximity tolerable as she wouldn't have in the past. That was Max's doing, as well. He'd taken the impish little dog in hand, just as he had everything else. She was so proud of Max. He was such a delight. It was simply too bad that Lissa and Max themselves . . . Well, she'd not get up her hopes in that direction. It wasn't hers to do. It was theirs.

Winding down, Aggie came to the place where she was to end the piece. Before it had a chance to crumble away on her, before Max had to prop it up with his baritone hum, she narrowed her eyes on the sheet of music and concentrated. When she applied her mind, the music invariably got better. Perhaps, on the next piece, she'd pay more attention to the notes than to the dancers on the floor.

"Well done, Aggie," Max called across the echoing room. "It amazes me that the waltz has barely caught on here. I understand it came into fashion only since the Peace Celebrations of last summer. They've been dancing the waltz on the continent for several seasons past."

"The patronesses only approved it last year," Aggie replied. "Although I can't say why, it's considered fast."

"You're surprisingly good at it," Lissa said, smiling at Max.

He grinned down on his smaller companion. "Probably because I'm something of a fast fellow myself."

Lissa chuckled and he went on, his voice wry. "I've never purposely led you to believe I'm totally lacking in social graces, you know. After all, wherever there's a Government House, there is almost always transported English society. Wherever we English go, we manage to take our tea and our ladies, and that means, at the very least, an occasional ball. A life following the drum is not entirely without the amenities. Not as the Upper Ten Thousand would have us believe. Now, Aggie," he said, "you must come dance with me."

"Yes, it's your turn," Lissa said.

"I'm afraid I'm not much improved," Aggie said, gathering her skirts nonetheless, "for all these past three mornings."

But Max didn't mind, and soon Lissa found herself sitting at the pianoforte, her eyes torn between the charming couple on the floor and the sheet of music on the instrument, just as Aggie had been before her. Max directed tender attentions to the elderly lady, which had her flushing with a pleasure that recalled her youth.

But Lissa had something else to distract her. A small marble statue of a female stood on the corner of the pianoforte, aligned so she could see it. That morning, Max had strode into the ballroom, a big smile on his face. Without preamble, he'd handed Lissa the statue. His gift, he'd claimed, was for the good she'd done him over the last few weeks. To Aggie, he'd presented bon bons.

And while Lissa had known she should refuse the statuette, because single ladies did not accept gifts from single gentlemen, Aggie and Max had insisted she keep it. And indeed, she wanted to keep it. She adored it already.

It was a small replica of the Medici Venus. With a grin,

Max had apologized for not giving her the genuine article. But then, he'd said, she would understand considering his financial pass.

All three had laughed. But Lissa had been touched that he'd remembered his promise to get her something. Not that she'd expected him to, but . . . well, she liked the statue very much. The Medici Venus was considered the ideal of feminine form and beauty, just as the long, graceful lines of the Belvedere Apollo were thought to best represent the male figure.

Puck's yap interrupted not only Lissa's musings but also her fingers, and then, in their turn, the dancers on the floor.

"I do beg your pardon," Boysen said from the open doorway. Lord Palmer was accustomed to running tame at Westmane House, and no one was surprised to see him there. " 'Tis a pity to interrupt such a delightful sight."

Lissa's heart sank. Puck jumped from his chair as if to go into his usual dither.

"Quiet," Max said. That was all it took. Puck meekly sat back down.

"Pray, come in, Palmer," Max called to Boysen. "We're just about to stop. The ladies have declared me fit for the dance floor. They don't expect I'll dirty too many slippers."

Boysen moved forward, all smiles. "Good morning, Lady Agatha. Pinkerton said I should find you here. I thought Lissa might like to drive out."

Lord Palmer bent over Lissa's hand, and she flushed with embarrassment. She wondered what Max would think if he knew of the secret engagement. She quickly put it from her mind. She would for as long as she could. As yet, it wasn't a comfortable *presentament,* although it surely would be shortly.

"I daresay *you* are preparing for Lady Daphine's come-out ball in particular," Boysen said.

"Indeed, it's upon us," Max replied affably.

"And your cravat, Your Grace. 'Tis much improved."

"I try." Max threw a meaningful look at Lissa.

At last, the visitor's gaze focused on what Lissa had been thinking she might hide, if given the chance. Still, it was too late. Boysen plucked up the statuette from the pianoforte. "And what's this? The Medici Venus?"

Max smiled with pleasure. "The very one. The lady who's drawn almost every aristocratic male in several past generations to visit her on their Grand Tour."

Aunt sniffed. "I daresay it's the lack of draperies."

While Lissa and Max chuckled at Aunt Agatha's quick reply, Boysen's smile dawned slowly. Lissa thought that his practice of *toujours la politesse* might save her yet. But no, he did have to ask. "Does it have some special meaning, standing here on the pianoforte this morning?"

"It's mine," Lissa said quickly.

But Max trod in. "I gave it to her this morning."

Lissa could see Boysen swallow hard. "You gave it to Lissa, Your Grace?"

Max's smile dimmed. "Is there something amiss in that?"

"T'isn't done," Boysen pronounced.

"T'isn't done?" Max inquired. When he thought Boysen ripe for roasting, he wasn't one to hold back.

"A gift from an unmarried gentleman isn't acceptable to an unmarried lady," Boysen explained, all courtesy.

"My stars," Aggie said to interrupt, her hand to her sagging red mane. "It was simply a show of gratitude on Max's part. There's no harm done."

Of course, Aggie was supposed to guard Lissa's reputation. And while Her Ladyship tended to bend the rules—to see some of the silly attitudes of the *haut ton* as just that—the baron did not bend.

"You must, with all due respect to His Grace, give it back, Lissa dear."

Max's smile disappeared. "Nonsense."

"No, no," Boysen insisted, not recognizing the light in Max's eyes. "It's obvious you don't understand. But now that the error has been pointed out, Lissa will return the statue. Even as well meant as the gift was intended, even as nice as it is, she will return it with all due respect."

Lissa saw Max regroup. "Here, now. This is deuced ridiculous. Damalis is my cousin. We are family."

Again, Boysen stubbornly held his ground. While he remained calm, even reasonable, he presented a hand, flat with protest. "I can see you don't understand, Your Grace. Even if you were true cousins, it would make no difference. In our society, the closest cousins can court and wed. And your addresses, even on the basis of your family connections, will never do. No, Lissa will return the Venus. As charming as it is, she will return it."

While Lissa had always known Boysen could be determined, his stubborn streak had never been so fully revealed. If both men hadn't seemed so entrenched in their positions, she would have laughed. Even Max was in earnest for a change.

Fortunately, Max backed down. He waved a large and negligent hand. "In the end, it's Damalis's to decide whether or not she keeps the statue."

Even as Lissa began to feel a wash of relief, Boysen spoke. "Oh, but I'm afraid you are far out there, Your Grace. Not that you would know, I see. And with all deference to an agreement I made with Lissa . . . Indeed, Lissa dear, you must forgive me, but—"

"No," she protested weakly. He couldn't. He wouldn't.

He did. "You see, Your Grace, I have every right to take this stand. Lissa and I are betrothed."

Certainly no room, whether large or small, could have

fallen more silent than did the ballroom at Westmane House. The proverbial pin could have dropped and sounded like thunder.

Exactly as Max said, "Be gad," Aggie whispered, "My stars."

No one could have been more surprised than Lissa's intimates. Her thoughts scrambled. She tried to explain; she wanted to take it all back . . .

But Boysen smiled. He was, despite his betrayal, excessively pleased with himself. "Really, Lissa," he said as if he hadn't betrayed her at all. "Having it out in the open is for the best. Yesterday afternoon, I visited Mama. She sees no reason to keep this a secret."

"But Boysen, we've . . . we've hardly decided ourselves."

"Come, come now. As my mama says, our betrothal will surprise no one. I've been acting as your escort to every London do for donkey's years."

Stepping up, Lissa took Aggie's hands. They felt cool. "I'm sorry you found out this way."

"Well," Boysen said, somewhat recalled. "Indeed, I didn't intend to shock."

Lissa's eyes turned to Max's. She didn't know what to say to him. If they'd been alone, she could have said what she wanted, though she wasn't sure what that was. But with Boysen looking on, with Boysen playing propriety, she said nothing.

In any case, Max had recovered. Striding to the bell rope, he gave it a short tug. "We shall have champagne. The best Pinkerton can unearth."

Lord Palmer appeared extremely pleased. "How kind of you, Your Grace."

"And I'll ask a favor, then."

"Yes?"

"In giving Damalis the Venus, I made the mistake, not she. Surely, if I've been brought to book, she should be allowed to have it."

"Well—"

"If we all keep it to ourselves, may she not keep it as an engagement present?"

Lissa could see how much against Boysen's grain the idea remained. Still, she thought it a good sign when he relented. He could bend a little, she told herself. He could see reason and consider the feelings of others. For a moment, she thought she had horribly misjudged him.

Unfortunately, things didn't improve after that. Whereas Boysen fully recovered, somehow Lissa didn't feel like celebrating. When they retired to the painted parlor, Max and Aggie listened, with every courtesy, to Lord Palmer. He explained his mother's thoughts on the wedding ahead.

It seemed they were to marry in the summer at Boysen's seat. In the meanwhile, Boysen and Lissa were to enjoy their engagement. Of course, it was understood there would be no big announcement ball. Balls were so very expensive. His mama had considered a quiet dinner *en famille*, instead. Perhaps, His Grace would be so kind as to oblige. While Lady Palmer despised London, as well as entertaining of any sort, she would, naturally, come up as soon as she could. She expected everyone would be very happy for Lissa and him—despite the nasty business concerning the Westmane estate. Which, of course, made no real difference to Boysen and his mama. Aside from a slight embarrassment, that was.

And finally, Lady Palmer in her own extreme delight had sent along her engagement ring to serve as Lissa's. It was part of the entail, in any case. It was too bad, however, that it was a bit large. Surely, a happy trip to Mr. Bridge would remedy that. Lady Palmer bought her diamonds from Mr.

Bridge. Just as did Her Majesty. Fortunately, her ladyship didn't live at such a distance from London that Mr. Bridge would not call on her. Just as he did for the Queen. Mr. Bridge would set the ring to right.

A trip to the jeweler was encouraged, even on the instant. Max and Aggie replaced near-to-full glasses of champagne next to Lissa's like glass on the heavily wrought and silvered tray that Pinkerton had brought in only a short time before.

That evening, a subdued trio entered the Westmane coach. While they felt, down to a person, that they'd done what they could to prepare Max for his first ball, for his first attempt at courtship, as always with the *beau monde,* there could be surprises.

Still, the evening began as expected. The Huntley Ball was a coveted invitation, and a veritable crush of carriages, chairmen, and boys with torches confronted them as they neared Huntley House in Hanover Square. Upon entering the house itself, moving up the staircase to the receiving line at its top, Lissa felt as if she'd been swept into a steady stream—a stream of bobbing feather headdresses, flashing jewels, and constant conversation.

Finally, they were met by Lord and Lady Huntley, posed as host and hostess for the glittering occasion, their prized jewel positioned between them. Looking at Daphne, Lissa recalled her similar first exposure to the *beau monde.* The girl was being fired off with every attention just as she had been. As everyone knew, the Earl of Huntley wanted titles for his daughters, and what better title could be had than the one Max had to offer?

Indeed, conjecture swirled about them. Lissa knew the *ton.* She also heard the whispered rush when Max bowed over the girl's hand. Daphne blushed, very charmingly.

She'd obviously been prepared for what was going forward and, once again, Lissa's heart went out to her.

Daphne was barely eighteen. Her skin was as white as the pearls that adorned her neck. Her hair was jet, her eyes large and dark, her smile pretty. She'd surely been told what to expect, but she was heartbreakingly young. And Max, despite his easy ways, must seem formidable.

Pushing on, the trio entered the ballroom. Boysen came forward, his biggest smile—which was no more than a ghost when compared to Max's—firmly in place. After his greetings for Lissa's companions, he was quick to inform them that their own good news was already making the rounds. As the evening progressed, Lissa could expect many happy felicitations.

Shortly, Aunt Aggie went off to join some friends, while Lissa remained with Boysen and her own friends. It amazed her to see just how happy everyone seemed to be for them. She would have enjoyed it more herself, she was sure, if only she hadn't had to keep an eye to Max.

She had to admit he did well. Smiling amiably, he met old comrades in the crowd, and was gradually introduced to some of the ladies. He began to dance and, once again, he did well. He certainly looked well. Lissa heard his name on any number of tongues.

And then, she was also complimented. She hadn't been in such good looks in a long time. Finally out of mourning, she wore one of her new gowns, an evening frock of amber *crêpe* over white satin with copper, metal-work trimmings.

Truly, everything couldn't have progressed more nicely.

Finally, Max led Lady Daphne out onto the floor. He seemed attentive without overwhelming the girl. Lissa sensed that he, too, was attuned to the girl's youth, to her inexperience and shyness. He smiled at her softly, and after delivering her to her mama, fetched her an orgeat. When

Lady Daphne smiled back at him, lowering her lashes in delicate shyness, the match was as much as made both in the eyes of the polite world, and the proud parents who stood looking on.

Lissa could hardly believe it had happened so quickly. But then, Max was a duke. She drew her first easy breath. She realized she'd been more concerned for his initiation into mixed company than she'd thought. When he came to claim his waltz with her, he smiled wickedly.

Sweeping out on the floor, the pair fell into their practiced harmony. Max grinned, relaxing into their relationship. "Well, how did I do?"

"From what I can tell—from what most everyone says— the match is made. My congratulations, Your Grace."

"It looks as if I shall make it by June eighteenth and better. You'd best prepare to pay up, Damalis." As he guided Lissa across the floor in large easy loops, his eyes were alight. Others made way, some even pausing to observe.

"The night is yours, Your Grace," Lissa said. "You've caused quite a stir."

"I have an excellent teacher. Perfect in every way. Except, that is, for her insistence on 'Your Gracing' me."

"I only 'Your Grace' you in public. It's right that I do."

"Ha! You do it to goad me, and we both know it. That may be the very forfeit I ask when I win our wager. That you never call me Your Grace again."

"That wouldn't be such a hard forfeit, Your Grace. I've been expecting far worse of you, Your Grace. Now, how could I have come to suspect you of demanding unfair spoils, *Your Grace?*"

Giving Lissa an extra swift turn, Max laughed down at her. "You'd best be careful, my girl. You may think you've made a tame cat of me, but don't be deceived by the cravat."

A delightful shiver struck Lissa's spine. "I don't doubt what you say for a minute, *Your Grace*."

The music ended, and tucking her hand beneath his arm in a way Lissa had to correct, Max guided her to the supper room. Boysen met them at the door. He fetched Lissa a plate from the buffet, just as Max did all that was correct by Lady Daphne. In fact, the four ended up seated together, along with some of Lissa's friends. But, once again, Lissa kept half an ear to Max's first real conversation with the earl's daughter.

Initially, it was hard going. Even for Max. Daphne's ball, her gown, her home in Suffolk were disposed of with only blushingly delivered monosyllables on the girl's part. The one safe topic appeared to be the flower arrangements. Unfortunately she thought he was talking about her cat. He was, of course, desperately referring to the roses and daisys as opposed to the cat. Still, one served as well as the other. Lady Daphne set off to describe Daisy's remarkable abilities and humorous antics. This longer discourse disclosed a charming lisp, a disposition as sweet as her appearance, and the care with which she'd been raised.

Talk of Daisy led to talk of her favorite sister, Lydia, and then to other sisters and their cats. Max was thus able to eat. All that was required of him was the occasional monosyllable on his part.

But Lissa's ears pricked up at a stammering mention of a younger son to a neighboring lord. His name was Simon, or "Thimon," as Daphne pronounced it so prettily. Lissa felt as romantically foolish as any girl of seventeen. Looking about, she saw that no one else took a like note of Daphne's frequent, lisping mention of "Thimon." Max was eating his syllabub.

Following dinner, the music resumed. Lissa was partnered by Boysen, and even by Max for a second waltz. Max danced again with Daphne, the final permissible dance, and then stood impassively by with Lissa to watch Daphne execute a country dance with Simon Tuttle.

Simon, a mere cub of twenty with the same jet hair as Daphne's, looked, at least to Lissa, a trifle forlorn and very Byronesque. But, once again, she saw this as a reflection of her own sentiments. She'd be glad when this season, that had hardly begun, was over. She'd be glad when they were all finally settled.

ℰℓ Chapter Nine

FOR ALMOST TWO WEEKS Lissa saw little of Max and much of Boysen. And then, at the end of those pair of weeks, Lady Palmer arrived. While Lissa, as well as Boysen, waited at Palmer House for three hours to greet her, Lissa had barely above ten minutes with the new arrival until her ladyship pleaded the necessity for seeking her bed with a lavendered cloth to her head. The journey, it seemed, had been too taxing. Not that Lady Palmer lived above an hour and a half from London, nor that her constitution didn't appear adequate to any trip.

But, all in all, Lissa's primary feeling was one of relief. She'd met her ladyship on two former occasions, both in London, both out in company and both years ago. It seemed unusual that the woman hadn't made more of an impression on her. But then, she hadn't been considering a possible relationship with the woman. Now she was overwhelmed.

And not by her physical dimensions alone—although those were more than adequate. Where Lord Palmer was slender and pale, Lady Palmer was robust and ruddy. She spoke with a loud voice. She thought that hers were the only opinions to be considered, and that surely everyone must know that. Her sentences fell like dictims, her whims like decrees.

Worse yet, Boysen acted the part of loyal Greek chorus. "Yes, Mama . . . Indeed, Mama." After a mere ten minutes, Lissa saw yet another side to the man she'd known for years, but who steadily became a stranger. His stubbornness was both born and bred of Lady Palmer's, and it deferred only to hers.

Glad for a respite from her weeks with Boysen, Lissa accepted an invitation from Lady Battersby. Despite the differences in their ages, Lady Battersby had always been one of her best friends. However, often of late, they hadn't seen one another—Lissa, because of her mourning, and Lady Battersby, because of . . . well, because of the usual. Judith had a large brood of children, only now growing into their own. That meant three children newly on the Town, and one daughter, Anabella, in her first season.

Lissa ended up at the old Battersby manse, which was not far outside of London, on a perfectly lovely afternoon. With its lawns sloping to a lake, it was the perfect setting for a family party. This particular party, obviously meant for the noisy and youthful company, was a treat for Lissa. The elder Battersby children, together with their friends, were represented in full force. Even some of the younger Battersbys dotted the crowd.

While Judith was busy, Lissa drifted out onto the terrace and onto the lawn. And there she spied Max. In his usual generous manner, he was filling two plates at the elaborate buffet. He surprised Lissa, however, when he turned and headed toward the linen cloths that had been spread on the grass—rather than to the collection of linen-draped tables where the adults sat.

Then she saw Daphne, seated on one cloth with two other young ladies and their equally young beaux. A smile came to Lissa's lips, all the while something bittersweet tugged at her. Max managed to get himself down and seated on the ground fairly gracefully—considering his booty from the buffet and his tight Corinthian clothing. But he next found it awkward to do anything with his long legs except to stretch them out.

Suppressing a laugh, Lissa retreated to a nearby garden, shaded her eyes with a gloved hand, and observed.

While the group about him laughed and chattered, Max simply ate in silence. Finished, he fetched two cut glass bowls of strawberries with clotted cream, and gingerly resumed his seat. Once settled, he realized he'd forgotten their spoons. Another trip for the silver, filigreed spoons proved too much for his patience. After fetching them he leaned down and handed one to Daphne, finally propping himself against a nearby tree to eat his dessert.

By the time the strawberries were served to everyone, games were announced on the open lawns. The more youthful members of the party raced off in eager anticipation. Since the season had begun they'd been tied to societal strictures. Now, their enthusiasm for the afternoon proved enormous, showing that Lady Battersby knew what she was about.

When Lady Daphne ran down the sloping lawn, in the company of young Simon Tuttle, Max stood, watching from the balustraded terrace. He'd obviously refused to join the games, and a small chuckle finally escaped Lissa's lips. He saw her then, sitting on a garden seat just below in the full-blown color of early spring bulbs. His face broke into an immediate and broad grin, and he started toward her, waving a hello.

Gratified, Lissa could read his genuine happiness at seeing her. She was especially glad she'd worn her favorite frock—a fluttery peach afternoon gown with ribbon knots and a matching, deeply-brimmed straw bonnet.

"You look like a flower yourself down here," Max said.

"I wish I had seen you sooner. Can I fetch you something to eat?"

"No, I ate before you did. For the last half hour or so I've been sipping at this tepid punch."

Max looked handsome in the sunlight. He was made for the out-of-doors, his large size at ease against the grander scale of open air and wide spaces. The sunshine that had colored his skin, became him. The breeze ruffled naturally in his hair, and his stride approached its most masculine grace on the uneven terrain. Lissa knew she'd never been so taken with him.

"You look lovely," he said, echoing her thoughts of him.

"Thank you, Your Grace."

"If you leave off 'Your Gracing' me, I'll offer my arm for a stroll. My legs need stretching."

"I'd like that."

Taking his arm, Lissa's heart fluttered. She felt as if she'd been given some special, brief reprieve. There was only this one day, in this single lovely spot. Best of all, Max seemed to feel the same. Patting her hand where it rested on his arm, he smiled down on her. "It's good to see you. It's been awhile."

They walked in silence, making a large lazy circle around the youngsters who played croquet. The laughter and banter, punctuating the sun-warmed air, mixed with sounds of birds calling and bees buzzing.

The older pair drifted along, brought out of their pleasurable silence by an unusually loud report of laughter. Glancing to the youthful group at the same time, they were drawn to Lady Daphne's slim figure. The girl stood watching the game, waiting her turn. Her attentions, like everyone else's were wrapped up in the frolicking males who were feeling their freedom.

"She's a lovely girl," Lissa said.

"Hmm?" Max murmured. "Oh, yes. A lovely little peagoose. Everything a man could want in a daughter."

Lissa's eyes turned to his in surprise. She expected a grin, but he wasn't teasing in this case. He was serious.

"Please," he said, his gaze sweeping the sunny spaces. "I need to talk to you. Over there," he added, indicating an ancient beech tree that stood out on the lawn as a shady retreat. "Let's take a minute and sit down."

Lissa followed, and upon reaching the deep shade beneath the tree, Max removed his coat and spread it on the ground. Lissa took her place on it, he dropping beside her, his large body lounging in its easy grace. The low-riding branches of the tree made the space fairly private. Even the sun reached through only in sharp rays that could pierce the thick foliage. One persistent beam shone on Max's now uncovered head, lighting the rainbow of colors that made up the chestnut hue of his hair.

"I've decided," he said softly, "that I can't marry Daphne."

Lissa, who was untying her bonnet, stared at him in disbelief.

"Don't look at me like that, my girl. No one could be more surprised than I am."

"But . . ."

Tugging a blade of grass from its place, Max began to wind it absently about a large index finger. "I'm four and thirty years old, Damalis. Lady Daphne is eighteen. I'm nearly old enough to be her papa."

"But it isn't unusual for gentlemen to wait as late as they can before giving up their freedom. Older gentlemen often marry young wives. Indeed, I think it's the fashion."

Max's smile shone wry. "Are you saying that we gents tend to be roués?" Lissa blushed and he went on. "Indeed, I've been told it's just the thing. To find a biddable little wife and bring her up, much like one does a child, to please oneself. But Lady Daphne is too young for me. Too far from my experience in every way. She's too much a creature of her own background to ever understand me. My past has made me what I am. Even maturity will never bridge the distances between us. She'll never speak of anything except cats and gossip and household concerns."

Lissa smiled. "But, Max. I think that's to be expected."

He wasn't smiling now. He remained sober. "I dare not tell anyone else this, but . . . Well, frankly, I want more. I've had a lot to think about here of late. I find that I want a home now. I've never had one, and being with you and Aggie has made me want one of my own. Going to Bowwood appeals to me immensely. I'll probably have to close up Westmane House for most of the time. At least, over the first years, while I concentrate on getting Bowwood together. Actually, I've come to like the idea. I want to be shot of town life. I want to do something constructive. I'm accustomed to being occupied. Even with funding from the earl, it'll take sacrifice. And no young girl like Daphne will like sharing the economies I'll have to practice until Bowwood is producing revenues again."

Max contemplated the green with which he'd striped his finger. Finally, he tossed the blade away. Lissa knew he was revealing his deepest self, and she waited until he went on to finish.

"I don't expect to fall in love. Indeed, I doubt there is such a condition. But I do want a meeting of the minds— some similar interests and some conversation. I want more than an heir. I want children. I want sons and daughters I can know and care for."

This was unusual talk for a gentleman. Most gentlemen left the rearing of their children to nursery staffs and schools.

Still, Max plunged ahead. "I know I'm asking a lot for the six weeks we have left. But I'd like to give it another try."

Lissa drew a peach-colored bonnet ribbon through her fingers. The light breeze reaching beneath the old tree rustled through the branches, the ribbons, the red of her hair. "The real concern," she finally said, "is removing yourself from the situation with as much grace as possible. Aunt and I have at least three more prospects to consider, so that's no worry. The heart of it is not to sully your reputation. Nor to hurt the Huntleys. They're truly nice people."

"Just so." Max squinted up his eyes against the brighter light beyond the shade of the tree. "I've made my attentions to Lady Daphne most marked. I've spoken to her papa . . . not finally, mind. I mean, I haven't proposed, as yet. But enough's been said for me to know the Huntleys would be happy with the match. Indeed, by every indication, Huntley would come down handsomely."

"It's such a shame," Lissa said on a sigh. "It's within your grasp—"

"But I cannot," Max said, with determination.

He looked over at the laughing players across the grass. "I especially don't want to crush Daphne. For all her innocence, she's awake on all counts with regard to me. She's, at least, somewhat proud of the prospect."

Lissa couldn't hide her sudden smile.

"Why do you find that amusing?" Max asked. "I wouldn't want to break the chit's heart."

"How overweening you are, Your Grace." While Lissa barely contained her wryest grin, Max looked truly puzzled. "Oh, I don't doubt," she admitted, "that Daphne was very proud to have such a handsome, titled, older gentleman dangling at her skirts. After all, she has sisters to laud it over. But, on the other hand, Your Grace, who does Lady Daphne speak of the most often?"

Max still tried to understand her playfully delivered point. "Her mama."

"And?"

"Daisy her cat. Her sister, Lydia."

"And?"

Understanding dawned. "Thimon Tuttle," he lisped in a gentle imitation.

When his gaze drifted to the group of youngsters, Lissa's followed. They had dropped their mallets and were dashing toward the collection of small rowing boats nudging at the shore of the lake.

"Well, I'll be damned," Max said under his breath. "How did you ever guess Daphne nurses a *tendre* for Simon Tuttle? You couldn't have been with her more than—"

"Once. You wouldn't know, of course, but I was very much like Lady Daphne at her age. I, too, was privileged and pretty and innocent. And also in love with a neighboring son."

Max's eyes softened with sympathy—a sympathy she once again found surprising. "I see," he said quietly. "I'm sorry, Damalis. You must have loved young Markham most sincerely."

Lissa realized, then, that Vernon Markham seemed a long distance away from her. She'd always thought her heart had gone with him to the grave, but . . . well, she wasn't so sure anymore. Wanting to ease the sympathy in Max's eyes, she groped for the thread of their conversation.

"Actually, Lady Daphne's *tendre* for Tuttle may be your way out of this."

"How's that?"

"Everyone knows that Daphne's the apple of her papa's eye. It would seem to me that the earl would want Daphne's happiness more than for her to be a duchess. *If* he could be brought around to seeing that. After all, Simon will be Sir Simon one day. Better a happy Lady Tuttle who lives on the marching estate, than an unhappy duchess who's forever complaining about her husband's being cheese-paring and away on his property all day."

Max grinned. "You paint a lovely picture of me as a husband. It's too bad I can't paint a like one for the earl."

"But that's precisely the point. You don't have to paint it."

Again he frowned.

"Aggie. She's bosom bow to Daphne's grandmama. We'll leave it to them."

"Gad. I hope they spare my blushes."

Lissa laughed.

Max attained his old self. "Damalis," he said, looking her in the eye, "if ever I've wanted to kiss you, and God knows I have, it's now."

Of course, Lissa knew better. But, oh, how she wished . . . Returning his dancing gaze, she sought for a jaunty reply that would turn them both—

Someone yelled. Indeed, several people called loudly from the area of the lake. Max was on his feet, reaching to pull Lissa up behind him. They ran down the gentle slope to see what was wrong.

The problem was quite clear. Several little rowing boats were out on the placid lake, each containing two passengers. An agitated clot of other children, including a wide range in ages, stood on the shore.

The boat that was farthest out contained Lady Daphne and her friend Anabella Battersby. It was filling fast with water, its rim barely above the surface. While Simon Tuttle already swam toward the boat, he'd forgotten that the young ladies would need a boat with which to be rescued. Indeed, he would no more reach them than he'd find himself not only without something into which he could hand them, but exhausted into the bargain.

Max immediately took action. Reaching the edge of the water, he tugged at his boots and shouted out a question. "Can anyone here row a boat?"

Lissa stood next to him, facing the group of youthful observers. Most of them appeared barely out of leading strings, their older relations obviously occupying the boats. The even older attendants hung about the terrace, still oblivious to the goings-on by the lake.

Max received no reply from the frightened faces before him. Only Lissa spoke. "I can row, Your Grace."

He appeared on the brink of refusing her. But, upon seeing the other possibilities, he swung her into a small vessel just at hand. He manned another. Within moments, they were smoothly and speedily making their way across the rippling surface of the lake. Lissa could barely believe what was happening. She was especially surprised to find she could still row fairly well. Only the sound of a seam giving way distracted her. A sleeve pulled away from the shoulder of her peach-colored gown. Still, she kept to her oars, her mind on the females in real distress.

Just as the lake waters breached the edge of Lady Daphne's boat, Simon reached a hand for her. Speedily the boat sank, leaving the girls sinking equally as fast. No one, except for a panting Simon, knew how to swim. The girls were terrified.

"All right now," Max called out. "Enough of the caterwauling. Mr. Tuttle, if you please. Grasp Lady Daphne about the waist and pull her to you. Put your other hand to Miss Westmane's boat. That will keep you both afloat, while I help Miss Battersby."

When Mr. Tuttle gripped Lissa's boat, Lissa noted the

sway. Staring into Daphne's wide, dark-eyed stare, she did what she could to reassure the girl while also keeping an eye to Max.

He'd already grasped Anabella's hand. He was both instructing her how to get into the boat and helping her, as well. It was an awkward business, to say the least. The small, two-person boats were not constructed for entry from water level. Max's boat nearly swamped twice, each time causing the terrified Miss Anabella to shriek.

"If you continue to scream, Miss Anabella," he said patiently, "we shall all end up deaf rather than drowned."

Miss Anabella stared at him saucer-eyed and then gave an extra effort. She plopped into the bottom of Max's boat, sodden clothes and all. Max righted her on the bench seat, his attentions already on the pair who waited, just outside of Lissa's reach. A quick reassuring glance at them showed her that poor Daphne's teeth chattered.

Maneuvering his own boat, Max was ready to assist the couple into Lissa's boat. "All right now, Tuttle. Don't be shy. Give Lady Daphne a good shove."

Simon licked his blue lips. "Yes, Your Grace."

Lissa didn't think anything could have been more awkward for the young pair. But Simon put what strength he had left to it, and soon both he and Lady Daphne crouched like half-drowned kittens, barely contained in Lissa's swaying boat.

"And now, Miss Westmane," Max said, as calmly as if he were asking her to take his arm for a quadrille, "we shall row as if the very devil is at our backs."

"Yes, Your Grace," Lissa said, as obedient as the others.

On her first stroke, Lissa's second sleeve came away from its seam. But she hardly noticed. Their charges were cold and wet, and she had all she could do to concentrate on the shoreline where a crowd had gathered. The nearer they came, the more relief took over. The tenseness that had held them in its grip was replaced by bravado. A few calls to Simon resulted in a general applause, then scattered praise for Max and Lissa.

Upon finally reaching shore, the girls were helped from the boats first. Max gave his final order. "Gentlemen. We'll have three coats for the ladies. And one, if you please, for Mr. Tuttle."

The two younger girls were soaked. Lissa realized her gown couldn't be all that was right, even if the rents were along her sleeves and shoulders. Soon, the group made its way back to the house that stood above on the rise.

Anabella Battersby was assisted by two chattering brothers, while Daphne leaned on Simon. Max and Lissa followed just behind the latter pair. Overhearing the conversation in front of them, their eyes met.

"Thimon, you thaved my life," Daphne said.

"Your life is more important to me than anything in this world, Daffy."

Max winked and Lissa smiled back. "Aggie and Daphne's grandmama will see to it," she said softly, only for him.

He nodded.

At the house, Lady Battersby took the same calm control Max had exhibited at lakeside. Baths were ordered for the three youngsters, and a fine Norwich shawl was fetched for Lissa. After her things were collected from beneath the beech tree, she had her coach brought around. She bid her hostess a warm farewell, and saw that Max had come to assist her into the Westmane carriage.

He smiled broadly now. "Damalis, my dear compatriot," he said, holding her in place just outside the coach door with a hand to her arm. "In the words of those young things with whom I have spent far too much time over the last two weeks, you are being touted as a great gun . . . a stout heart. Still, I couldn't put it better myself."

Lissa smiled up into his honeyed gaze. "You are all that is kind for saying so, Your Grace."

ℒ *Chapter Ten*

"PRAY, LISSA DEAR," Boysen said in an undertone, "you must not fidget with your engagement ring. You know how it disturbs Mama."

"I apologize, Boysen. I'm unaccustomed to it. And then, it's so large."

"*Large?*" he repeated, a tad offended. "But we've had it sized."

Fortunately, just then the doors of the formal drawing room at Palmer House were flung wide and Lissa rose to her feet. She and Boysen had been waiting nigh onto twenty minutes, much as one would wait for an audience with the Queen. If the old Queen gave audiences for strictly social purposes, which she did not.

"Ah, Lissa dear," Lady Palmer said, offering Lissa two fingers to curtsy over. "I'm glad you are here. We have much to discuss. And how excessively nice my . . . I mean, *your* ring looks on you. True, your hand is a bit small. It doesn't quite do justice to a ring of that size. Not as mine did. But, as I was telling my son, it's the sentiment that counts."

Before Lissa could reply, her ladyship had turned away to seek her chair by the fire. A late spring chill was in the air, and Lady Palmer had wrapped up in two shawls. She was a large woman, but the shawls made her seem enormous.

Boysen joined Lissa on the sofa, while his mother continued to adjust her shawls.

"I shall be happy to turn this house over to you, Lissa dear. The drafts here are something dreadful. But you, however, must be accustomed to them, what with living at Westmane House."

Lissa looked to her fiancé. She thought he might have said something, but he merely cleared his throat. He'd mentioned his nose being ticklish.

"In any case," her ladyship said, "I have the headache. Still, I also know there are things we must discuss. Firstly, about the little engagement party I suggested, you recollect, in lieu of an announcement ball. While we will, quite naturally, miss the excitement of our friends felicitating us, we can do without a ball very nicely. We realize that, what with your embarrassing financial position, Lissa dear, some sacrifices will have to be made. And we'll share them cheerfully, will we not, Boysen?"

"Yes, Mama."

"That's very kind of you," Lissa said. "And while the duke did offer a ball, I refused his kind offer. There's no sense in spending where we need not. Even so, he will be happy to have us to dinner. He extends his invitation to you through me, fresh from his breakfast table."

"So, you have breakfast with His Grace, then?"

Lissa had to think as to how to reply. She didn't want to leave the impression that she and Max were in each other's pockets, which, of course, they weren't. She'd seen little of Max since the Huntleys' party three weeks earlier.

Nor did she want the Palmers to realize how informal Max could be.

On the other hand, she thought they should know how sincerely his invitation had been made. She could still see the grin that had spread into his face when she'd mentioned such a possibility. "Out to do the pretty by the in-laws, are we, Damalis?" he'd asked.

"Well," Lady Palmer intoned, "I daresay, His Grace is most considerate. Indeed, we shall be happy to accept his invitation. You must understand, however, that my two daughters, who would like to be included, are . . . well, suffice it to say, they are in interesting circumstances."

Lissa knew those circumstances. The one sister had recently given birth while the other awaited that event. "Whoever can come, shall be welcome," she said. "Why don't you correspond between you? You can then tell me a date that will be convenient for everyone."

"And that would be acceptable with His Grace?" her ladyship inquired, as if she couldn't believe her ears.

"Oh, yes. His Grace is very agreeable."

"He sounds lax to me," Lady Palmer declared. "And what are His Grace's views as to the wedding itself?"

Even though Lissa had never broached this subject with "His Grace," she knew she could answer for Max. She'd decided to satisfy her ladyship first. Max would fall in with whatever plans they made. "He thinks the wedding sounds delightful," Lissa lied, trying to pacify this virago.

"His Grace sounds too amiable." Lady Palmer's gaze pierced into Lissa's. "Perhaps, His Grace is too unaccustomed. After all, he can't know much about being a duke. A gentleman, particularly one of his standing and responsibilities, should take a firm hand. Boysen is a perfect example. There's no real urgency for my son to marry so young. He's but two and thirty. And yet, he knows he must. While he has heirs in his sisters' children, they're not Palmers. And we'll settle for no less than a Palmer for the barony, will we not, Boysen?"

"Yes, Mama. I mean, no, Mama. We'll settle for no less."

"It's a dreadful shame, what with the Westmane line having been broken. What's this person's name? Jameson, is it not?"

Lissa bridled, but held her tongue. To think that she'd actually shared the judgments these people regularly made now revolted her. "Yes, his name is Jameson."

"See what I mean, Boysen? A Scot, no less. We'll have none of that in our time."

"No, Mama. None at all."

"This whole business has been shameful," her ladyship repeated. "All that money wasted. Boysen has told me about your own funds, Lissa dear."

"Yes, ma'am."

"But then, fortunately, that doesn't matter with us. We're after good blood. And, as anyone can say, there's no blood finer than your own, dear Lissa. Blood tells."

"Yes, ma'am." *Oh, lud,* she sounded like Boysen. Was there no one who stood up to this harridan?

"Of course, I'm happy the whole business—the marriage, I mean—will be dispensed with quietly. I'm anxious to see Boysen settled before I go off to Yorkshire this summer. I have a sister in Yorkshire, and she's forever asking me to visit. She knows I detest traveling the distance, but I shall go. We all have our duties. And now, I shall leave the pair of you to your tea. I would take it with you, but I'm worn to a shade. What is it, Boysen?"

Lissa looked over in time to see her intended's weak signal to his mother, and her ladyship resettled on her chair. "I'd nearly forgotten, Lissa dear. Just one more matter. Boysen says you are to go to the Things for a few days."

"Yes, we are."

"All of you?"

"Well, what there is of us. My aunt, His Grace, and myself."

"I daresay His Grace is interested in meeting Sir Cornelius's daughter."

"As a matter of fact, he is."

"They live not far from me, you know."

"I didn't realize—"

"It's of no consequence. I don't know the Things. Not that I haven't heard of them, mind. But then, His Grace is looking for money, where we are looking for blood."

Lissa didn't reply. She didn't need to. Her ladyship could carry a conversation by herself. But then, her ladyship wouldn't want to. Her joy in conversing arose from having at least one person to bully. Lissa wondered if all of Lady Palmer's children had been reduced to parrots with a single word vocabulary: "Yes."

"What I'm trying to say, Lissa dear," her ladyship said, more confidentially. Her large face, with its large features came closer. "I don't think it proper you go along to the Things."

"But Pru— I mean, Miss Thring is my friend. I suggested her name to His Grace. I don't understand."

"From what I hear, Sir Cornelius's house is most lax."

"Lax?"

"There is no companion for Miss Thring. There hasn't been since the girl's governess-companion passed away over three years ago."

Lissa knew this was true. "But my aunt is going with me."

"Still," her ladyship drawled, with a pursed look that was almost ludicrous, "Sir Cornelius is unmarried."

"But—"

"And so is that son of his, Finchley."

"Yes, but they're very nice. I've stayed with Pru before."

"Without a lady to watch over you?" Her ladyship appeared aghast. No, more a caricature of that expression. Irreverently, Lissa pictured Thomas Rowlandson—one of three great Caricaturists—executing her beefy features, her overblown mannerisms, to perfection.

"I was only a girl when I visited," Lissa managed. "But Pru's governess and her mama were with her, then. The Thrings were friends to my late grandparents, who lived—"

"I see," Lady Palmer said. She tapped a thick finger to a bulbous lower lip. "Even so, I cannot approve. It hardly seems right that you go off to a house party, no matter how brief, when your own fiancé isn't invited."

Lissa didn't know what to say.

"Of course, if Boysen could somehow be invited . . . And then, if you'd insist, I could come along, I suppose. It would seem entirely all right, then."

"But I don't see how I can ask."

"Oh, asking is no problem. Not when you say Miss Thring is your friend."

Truly, Lissa didn't know how to reply. And Boysen . . . well, Boysen was helping his mother up from her chair, even escorting her to her room. What could Lissa say to vacated space?

Still trying to decide what to do on the following morning, Lissa arose early and sought out her aunt in the breakfast parlor. At her place there was a note from Boysen. It didn't help matters. Nor did the fact that Aggie was nowhere to be found. In taking her chair, Lissa was alone with Max.

Not that he lacked entertainment. Max received numerous newspapers as well as much correspondence from across the channel. When she put down her note from Boysen, Max peered at her, a letter in his square fingers.

While he seemed serious, he smiled at her readily enough.

"Aggie's gone to sit with that ladyfriend of hers who's ailing," he said, as answer to her question. "Mrs. Maypost."

While it was as cool outside as it had been on the previous day, the sun glistened in through the windows of the parlor, revealing every detail of the delicate, French furnishings.

"Is something wrong?" Lissa asked.

He looked as if he might smooth the matter over, despite the newspapers and the scattering of letters. "I suppose I can tell you," he replied. "I wouldn't say if Aggie were here, but—"

"What is it? Brussels?"

"It looks grave. Bonaparte is mustering his forces again. I have an especially good friend over there now. The crossing's only twelve hours, so we can write regularly. He's worried, and I trust him to know. Whatever happens, it'll be a close-run thing."

Lissa saw that her own problems paled in comparison to this. Max interpreted her look, because he reached across the space between them and patted her hand. "We have some wonderfully fine men over there, Damalis. If anyone can do it, it's they. Each one is worth a dozen of the men milliners we see here. We have a damned good chance, so don't fret. In any case, whatever happens, it's probably weeks off."

"I suppose you're sorry you can't be there."

"I was good at soldiering," he said honestly. "And they'll need every good man they can lay a hand to. But no, while part of me still responds to the duty, I don't seek the glory anymore. My heart has turned to home now. There's a duty to be done here, as well. A duty no one else can do. And one I've come to . . . well, to accept with an odd sort of relish. If I could find a wife—" He smiled at her more gently. "As I've said, you've become my friend, Damalis. And then, you were the one to suggest Miss Thring. Aggie gave me the dates of our invitation."

"Pru responded quickly to my letter. And don't worry that I hid my teeth. She and I have known each other since the cradle. Of course, I haven't seen her in years—since our come-out season—and I suppose that's why I didn't think of her sooner. I know you'll like her, though. And she certainly has a lot in common with you. She, too, loves the country. She lives with her father and brother, and they spend all the time they can outdoors. She's a bruising rider, and a good conversationalist. Something I know you'll appreciate. She's my age—"

He grinned. "An ape-leader, eh?"

Lissa had learned to smile back. "The Thrings are very nice, very *handsome* people. As I recollect, they look fresh from the out-of-doors."

When Max's eyes caught her fiddling with her engagement ring, Lissa dropped her hands to her lap. The ring was a great, gaudy thing, a combination of stones and filigree that weighed down her hand. Trying to ignore both it and Max's seeking, sherry eyes, she went on. "Sir Cornelius, Pru's father, is a good-hearted man. He's only one step removed from trade, however. That doesn't bother you, does it, Max?"

"I daresay if the duchy can stand the son of a don for its duke, it can tolerate the granddaughter of a tradesman for a duchess."

"That's what Aggie said. Of course, Pru has her own fortune, as well as what her father will certainly offer. Pru—short for Prudence in this case—is a wonderful catch."

Max smiled. "It sounds as if everything's in train. And

I," he said, his smile deepening the lines about his eyes, "have a surprise for you."

"Oh no, Max. No more gifts. I—"

"Never say a gift," he added to her protests. "This is more—well, run abovestairs and put on something warm. We're going out."

"Actually, it's very kind, but I don't have time to—"

"That won't wash, my girl." He waited at the door of the breakfast parlor, holding it open for her. "Downstairs. Entryway. Ten minutes."

Lissa couldn't help her dry smile. "Is this an order, Your Grace?"

"Very definitely. And you, my dear Damalis, are to step lively."

"Your men must have disliked you."

"Excessively."

In fact, Lissa had a jaunty costume from a few years past. An especial favorite, it caused hope to flicker in Stowe's eyes when Lissa entered her chamber calling for it. Perhaps, the mistress would start dressing again—dressing in a style that had rivaled any lady of the *ton* when that outfit had been new.

Lovingly pulling the costume from the cupboard, Stowe soon had Lissa ready to go. A navy-blue spencer, decorated *à la militaire*, topped a white gown. An equally provocative shako, complete with a red plume and gold braid, was placed on quickly arranged curls. Even so, Lissa was right on time, and Max swung wide the front door. There, in the curve of the drive, a curricle and pair—a black pair with matching stockings and blazes—waited with a groom from the stables.

Lissa's heart plummeted.

But Max already had her arm. "Come now, Damalis. You look fine as five pence. I won't let you go back to your room in retreat. Besides, anyone who can row a boat as coolly as you did the other day can drive a curricle and pair."

"No, Max. I can't," she whispered hoarsely.

He softened somewhat. "Yes, you can. You've got bottom. You're named for it, remember? My little soldier."

Still, Lissa balked on the stone staircase. She was glad no one but the single groom and the pair of stamping blacks saw the fear in her eyes.

"I've had some sticky times myself, my girl." Max spoke at her shoulder, his hand still at her elbow. "Sometimes you have to throw your heart over and follow it. In any case, I'll be with you. If I must, I know enough to take the reins."

Without deciding to, Lissa moved forward. The groom steadied the horses while Max assisted her up. With the very first sway of the carriage, she expected the old dread to overwhelm her.

But it didn't. Gingerly, she took the reins. Max sat beside her, and at his signal, the groom let go. The horses were ready. More than ready. Lissa had to catch up quick. But, as with the rowing, it felt as if she'd never stopped. No one could have guessed it had been ten whole years.

They were down the drive in an instant. The old skills came back. Expertly she turned onto Piccadilly, certainly one of the worst thoroughfares for driving. But Hyde Park waited nearby and, with another neat maneuver, she guided them onto its safer roadways. Even so, she didn't take her eyes from the rush of oncoming pavement. Nor did she hold the ribbons lightly . . .

Lightly. She could hear that. In Vernon's tones. And as if he were smiling at her. They'd been as close as . . . as . . . Suddenly, it struck her. They'd been as close as brother and sister. Brother and sister.

Daring to look away from the horses' rumps, if only for a moment, Lissa glanced at Max. He grinned.

"You're doing it, my girl. I knew you could."

Lissa smiled weakly, her eyes flying to her horses and the oncoming tilbury. Finally, the real blow had been landed. She'd received, as the gentlemen who followed the Fancy would say, her leveler. She hadn't loved Vernon Markham any more than as a brother. She knew that now, because she'd finally fallen in love. And her love for Vernon didn't approximate what she felt for Max.

How could he not know? she wondered, taking another quick glance at Max. Sitting as he was, his eyes switching from the roadway to her and back, he was so obviously ignorant. And it was so obviously clear. How could he not know? The only reply was that he didn't.

Drawing a deep breath, Lissa lightened her hold. Concentrating, she got the feel again. Yes. It was all right again. It was a joy again. Driving was easy when compared to falling into unrequited love. Even if she hadn't been engaged to Boysen, it wouldn't have made any difference. Even if Max didn't need a rich wife, he wouldn't have looked to Lissa for an attachment. Sadly, the man she loved was not in love with her. He'd said, twice, that he doubted he would ever experience love. So, what did her love matter?

She took one more look at him.

Max smiled, his voice proud. "Next time out, you'll teach me. I want to do this as well as you do it."

Lissa didn't reply. Not until they spun into the drive, where she feathered a curve to the inch and pulled to a stop as neat as wax. Trying to remain aloof, she let Max help her down. With an effort, she gathered her wits. She had to go on with this season, now more than ever. She had to get herself out of Max's house, out from under the feet of his

bride. She had to help him win his bride. She felt desperate
to do so.

"*Mon brave*," he said, chucking her on the chin.

"Max," she replied, bringing him to full attention as they
broached the entryway. Once again, only the gladiator stood
watch. "I'm sure you remember my mention of an engagement dinner party. For just the two families."

He nodded.

"Is the evening after tomorrow all right?"

"Isn't that the night before we leave for the Thrings'?"

"Yes. I'm afraid things are moving more quickly than I
would have thought. Boysen sent around a note this
morning. He's inquiring about that night in particular. It
seems his mother wants to have this dinner in order to meet
you before . . . before they accompany us to the
Thrings'."

"What? The Palmers are going to the Thrings'?"

"I'd rather not explain now. When you meet Her Ladyship, it will come clear."

"Gad," he said, realization breaking. "But, of course,
whatever you say. Dinner in two nights. I'll be there."

"And would you mind . . . I mean, would you come
down a little early?"

His smile was ready. "Need moral support, eh?"

"As much as I can garner."

"I'll be there. That's what friends are for."

There. He'd said it. He saw them merely as friends.

✁ *Chapter Eleven*

LISSA KNEW she looked pale. Hoping to give herself some color, she donned a rose-colored gown with rose velvet trimming. Rose net was worn over a white satin slip, while the rose velvet made up the small, puffed sleeves and the long ribbon at the high waist. She also had Stowe take some time in arranging a difficult coif consisting of tiny braids, tight curls, and more rose ribbons. That done, she pinched some color into her cheeks and turned from the mirror over her toilette table.

Behind her, high on a shelf was the statuette Max had given her. Sometime soon, she'd have to pack it away because it would offend Boysen. In the meanwhile, she'd try to wean herself from its cheering presence.

Not that it was exactly the thing. After all, the Venus was nude and, perhaps, blushingly so. Still Lissa liked it, and it would be a sacrifice to hide her away. But then, there would have to be other sacrifices. She'd begin to make them this very night. Squaring her shoulders and pinching her cheeks one final time, she headed for the painted parlor. Everything was set for the engagement dinner party even with their substantially reduced staff. Cook had been preparing an elaborate meal all day, and Lissa could rely on Pinkerton to see to the serving.

When she entered the painted parlor, Lissa was a bit disappointed that Max wasn't there yet. She expected the evening to be an ordeal. Lady Palmer had sent a note saying that, while her daughter Beatrice would be unable to attend, it appeared that Carola would be happy to share in their joy. Carola had come up to London, particularly for their evening of celebrations.

Tempted to check the color in her cheeks yet again, Lissa was grateful when Max came in. He now seemed adapted to the attire of the fashionable town gentleman, although tonight he wore pantaloons and tied shoes with his blue coat, rather than the more conservative knee breeches, silk stockings, and evening pumps. In any case, he looked as wonderful to Lissa as always. Soon, she'd have to wean herself from even his simplest company, as well.

"My little Trojan," he said, with a grin.

"Not so brave tonight."

"And thus I've come to read you your marching orders."

"Actually, I need to speak to you about something which is very important."

"You do, in truth, seem grave."

"I don't look too pale?"

He examined her face. "Perhaps, a bit pale. But surely this Tartar hasn't brought you to your knees."

"She's excessively formidable."

"Even so, you'll come about. Think of yourself addressing me on the occasions when we first met. That should put starch in you."

Lissa's eyes dropped. "That's unfair, Max. I've apologized for that—tried to make it up."

"Sorry, my girl. You have done. Let me deal with the dragon. I've been trained to slay dragons, you know."

"No, no. That's precisely what I want to speak to you about. Oh, don't give me your wary look. It's not you, it's . . . Oh, Max. If you continue to poke at Boysen, he's sure to take offense sooner or later."

Another smile. "He hasn't caught on yet. What makes you think he ever will?"

There. The point Lissa was trying to make. Still, Max looked so marvelous with that wicked smile, that keen intelligence behind it. Suddenly, foolishly, tears welled up in Lissa's eyes. She hadn't cried in years, and yet, she couldn't . . . well, she couldn't cry now.

But Max saw. Stepping up to her, he took her into a comforting embrace. "Here, here, now," he said, softly. "It'll be all right. It'll come 'round. You'll see."

"But what I want to ask you—"

The door of the parlor opened, halting Lissa's words. Max stepped back, looking, along with her, to the motionless figure hovering in the doorway. Boysen cleared his throat, his eyes wide.

"Here, here, old fellow," Max said, moving away from Lissa altogether. "Don't poker up, so. I was only helping Damalis remove a mote from her eye. It's out now, is it not, Cousin?"

Tugging a handkerchief from her sleeve, Lissa wiped the few remaining tears. "Yes, thank you. It's out now."

Boysen straightened his slim shoulders. For a moment, Lissa thought he might not accept their excuse. Still, he was motivated by all that was polite. "I've come ahead. With Mama. She waits below in the carriage. We thought we should inform you that my sister will not be dining, after all. I knew you would like to rearrange the table. Indeed, my sister sends her most sincere regrets."

"*Neither* sister is well?" Max inquired. "I hope they're not sickening with something."

"No," Boysen replied coolly, as if he considered Max a

dolt. "Ladies in their condition are often plagued by indisposition."

Max had no way of knowing one sister had recently given birth, while the other soon would.

"Pray, don't concern yourself, Your Grace," Lissa explained. "While one sister just had a child, the other continues in a family way. Under the circumstances, it's not unusual to need one's rest."

"Ah, well. How wonderful and how unfortunate. But I suppose we'll soon learn those lessons ourselves. How good it is, Palmer, that you're somewhat prepared, what with having sisters. I shall be dreadfully ignorant when my turn comes."

"Dreadfully ignorant of what, my dear?" Aggie swept into the room only to catch sight of Boysen and sober. "My stars. Am I late?"

Lord Palmer bowed. "No, Lady Agatha. My mama and I are somewhat early."

"Oh, well, then, that's good. And what was it you were saying, dear Max?" Lissa had hoped to drop the subject, but Aggie stood waiting for an answer. "I'm sorry I interrupted you."

"I was only saying I don't know a single thing about babes. Nor, of their mamas, for that matter."

"Well," Aggie sighed. She was both spinster and expert. "From what I understand, it's all very natural."

Lissa could see that Boysen, already offended, didn't care for this easy conversation. He frowned. "I think this subject unsuitable, especially for the ladies."

"What precisely is it about babes and their mamas that you find unsuitable, Palmer?" Lissa could see the light of devilment spark in Max's amber eyes.

"There's nothing about them which is intrinsically improper. However, it's unseemly to discuss such things in company."

Max's eyes burned brighter. "Now, don't you think that odd of our society? On the one hand, it's only possible to attain the particular state about which we speak in mixed company, and yet, we cannot talk about it in mixed company."

"Your Grace," Boysen said, all starch. "I realize you are largely without experience—"

"Oh, my!" Lissa said, grasping at straws. "How can we have forgotten your mama? Indeed, Boysen, she cannot be comfortable in the carriage."

"She said she would do."

"Oh, but we must make amends. Please, Your Grace, and dear Aunt. Let's extend our hopes for a quick recovery to Boysen's sisters, and rush to make Lady Palmer feel welcome."

Did she actually say those words? Lissa was sure she was approaching hysterics. Still, they seemed to suffice. The quartet moved out of the painted parlor and in the direction of the grand staircase.

Max's smile to Lissa said he was awake on all counts, but she knew he wasn't. She hadn't made him promise to behave himself, if only for her sake. She had horrible visions of the evening ahead.

And in the entry those visions began to solidify. When Boysen went to fetch his mama from the carriage, Aunt Aggie and Lissa had a harried exchange. Max and the bronze gladiator looked on, all confidence. Rather than rushing into the formal atmosphere of the State Drawing Room, Lissa tried to regroup in the entry.

"'Tis all right to greet her here," Aggie insisted in a hurried whisper.

Lissa's whisper rang huskily through the large space.

"But it's not precisely the thing. And you know, Aunt, what a stickler Lady Palmer is."

"Goodness, yes I do. A more badly tempered female—"

"Aunt!" Lissa said to hush her, her eyes warning Max as well. "Pinkerton is opening the door."

And so they stood, like good soldiers, directly in line with the gladiator. Lissa forced a smile. Her plans had been ruined. She wasn't certain she could get everything back in train until they entered the State Drawing Room. Surely, even Lady Palmer would be impressed by that room. Surely, Lissa hoped, her ladyship would be somewhat subdued on such impressive ground.

And then, in she trod, her weighty gown and double shawls, her large jewelry, a challenge even to the ponderous lair of the Westmanes. In addition to her usual costume, Lady Palmer wore a plum-colored turban with gold braid twisted through it. The latter ended in a pair of dangling tassels which swayed with every step.

After accepting the introductions her son made as her due, her ladyship paused. Her eyes ran the gladiator, and Lissa's pulse began a slow throb in her head.

"What's this?" Her voice boomed up into the very rafters of the house.

Lissa licked her dry lips. "Why, that's been in that very spot since—"

"Yes," her ladyship drawled disapprovingly. "I can imagine. Burlington and Kent. I've seen some of their other rooms. One must have been half-mad and the other half-perverse. All those ugly creatures that are part person and part heaven knows what. And then, this fascination with-
. . . well, with indecency. I should have this stored, Lissa dear. As soon as may be. Your uncle is gone now, and it's your duty to see to it that such changes are made. You should have told her so sooner, Boysen."

"Yes, Mama."

Thinking of nothing except moving Lady Palmer into the State Drawing Room, Lissa all but grabbed the woman's elbow. "Pray, you must come sit by the fire, my lady," she said, avoiding Max's eyes altogether.

"Indeed, after that cold carriage, a fire sounds pleasant. But then, there's no hearth like one's own hearth. That's what I always say."

They all settled on chairs that arced the fireplace of the State Drawing Room below the intricate chimneypiece.

"I understand, Your Grace," Lady Palmer said as an opening salvo, "that you gave Lissa a gift of a small statue."

Lissa almost groaned aloud.

"Yes," he said simply.

"While I'm sure that was most considerate of you, I hope Boysen has made it plain that it isn't done."

"He did."

"That statue, I understand, is also without draperies."

"It is."

Finding no heat there, her ladyship turned to Lissa. "You will have to pack it away as well, my dear. Perhaps, someday when your children are grown, you may display it again. You see, I do understand it is a piece of *art*. But these pieces of *art* do not suit in family settings."

As the evening wore on, it grew worse. Even Aggie withdrew behind a prunish look that Lissa knew kept her from making an unkind remark.

Max observed the Amazon lazily, avoiding conversation altogether. While his smiles for Lissa were reassuring, she knew he was repelled by the Palmers. As he refrained from making his subtle points with Boysen, she had to be grateful.

At dinner, the tassels on Lady Palmer's turban jiggled

with every large bite she took. She proclaimed the pigeon wrapped in bacon overdone, and she had a far better receipt for apple panada from Lady Wooster. Her ladyship, Lady Wooster, that was, might be persuaded to share her receipt. She was such a fine lady, and Lady Palmer, who lived barely a mile from her, had much influence with the woman.

And while the Westmane set of Waterford was excellent, Lady Pockington had a beautiful and extensive set of crystal. And then, of course, the Palmers owned a cupid by Sèvres that was beyond compare. That had to be admitted by anyone. "Is that not true, Boysen?"

"Indeed, Mama."

Finally, Max interrupted. He looked entirely serious. "And this Sèvres cupid, my lady. Is it clothed?"

"Why don't be silly, Your Grace. Cupids, the darling creatures, are hardly ever clothed. Not with much, in any case."

"And do you like cherubs?" Max inquired.

"Why, everyone knows cherubs are quite as charming as cupids. I was only now admiring the cherubs which adorn the frieze in this very chamber."

"Well, if nude cherubs are more to your taste, I'm sure you would appreciate the Duchess of Westmane's bed. On sleeping there one night, I counted no less than twenty of the naked little devils, cavorting from headboard to foot-post. I'd be most happy to show you the bed, my lady."

Lady Palmer declined Max's invitation. At this point she suggested the ladies withdraw. *Unbelievably*, Lady Palmer was in rout.

"Pray, Lissa dear, you must lead us away," she said. "The gentlemen should be left to enjoy their own conversation."

Lissa felt that, at last, some justice would be meted out.

While she might have to endure Lady Palmer's company over tea in the State Drawing Room—with Aunt Aggie glowering on—His Grace would be left with Lord Palmer, who was even now excusing himself for a string of sneezes. Max had merely removed a cigar from an inner pocket.

Surely, nothing could be worse than this evening. Not even the threat of the following morning, when the same company would climb into coaches and make their way to the seat of the Thrings, just outside St. Albans in Hertfordshire.

♫ *Chapter Twelve*

LADY AGATHA WESTMANE was worried about Lissa. Despite her trim pelisse of lilac, figured sarsenet and the fabric lilacs in her bonnet, the gel looked a bit peaky. She had done for several days. But then, who wouldn't be off their looks? Lissa and Puck and herself were stuffed into a single carriage with Lady Palmer and Lissa's dresser, Stowe, who was as starchy as a linen napkin.

Behind them, in the Palmer Town chariot, Boysen followed with his man, Pinseat. The old Palmer traveling coach brought up the rear with Lady Palmer's woman and the groaning load of baggage. One would have thought that such an impressive entourage was going far afield and for days on end. They merely traveled to St. Albans, however, and then off the Great North Road.

Max, who had chosen to go by horseback along with his bathman, Bagley, circled back upon occasion to peer into the coach and tip his hat. Lissa was the subtle focus of his attentions, and as always, Aggie found his teasing address charming. Max looked his best on horseback. His stallion, Pegasus, a great cream-colored beast, suited him like a glove to a hand. Max was, in truth, the single relief in the tedious affair.

Even now, as he guided Pegasus up alongside the

carriage. He lowered his large frame so as to peer in and smile, first at her, and then, more broadly at her niece. Surprisingly, Lissa pulled her nose just the slightest bit at him, and he moved off with a chuckle. Poor, dear girl. Lady Palmer's complaints and comparisons ran like a continuing stream. Even Puck, poor creature, looked a bit peaky. He sat on Lissa's lap, directly across from Aggie.

"Here, Lissa. Let me take him for a while," Aggie said, leaning forward with outstretched hands.

When Lissa didn't respond for a moment, Aggie decided something was either seriously amiss with her niece, or that Lady Palmer's voice had driven her into her own thoughts.

Finally, Lissa signaled with a wan smile and Puck was passed to Aggie's hands. "There, now," she said to him, finding her sympathy for the old Pekingese as startling as Lissa obviously did. "We haven't much farther to go."

Shortly after Aggie spoke, Max rode back as proof of her assurance. Smiling, he tipped his hat and lowered himself so he could look at Lissa. In this instance, she ignored him altogether.

"Just ahead now, ladies."

"Oh," Lady Palmer pronounced. "Can it be true!"

Lissa finally glimpsed the low, rambling structure of Hunt Hall. Originally it had belonged to the Modley family, but, when Sir Cornelius had come into his own and the Modley fortunes had reversed, he'd bought the estate which consisted of hundreds of acres of largely unspoiled and unfarmed land. Sir Cornelius, as Lord Modley before him, used the acreage for amusement. Here, the Things, like the genteel family before them, followed the change of seasons. They shot in the fall, hunted during the winter, and fished and rode through the warmer months. Here, they entertained similar friends with marching interests. Here, London's round seemed far away.

While it had been years since Lissa had visited the hall with her grandparents, the place retained its flavor. She remembered her last visit as an easy time, unscheduled and unhurried. She looked forward to seeing Pru. And then, once again, she was determined to get through this horrible season with its equally painful purposes. Pru, indeed, seemed just the girl for Max.

Finally, the cavalcade pulled into the graveled drive and stopped. In London, or even on any well-organized estate, they would have been met by an immediate rush of retainers, coming to hold the horses and direct the baggage. But, even as Lissa escaped the confines of the Westmane carriage, even as the horses' gear jingled in her ears, she knew the pace had fallen off. Looking at her numerous companions, seeing them shake out their clothing and seek to the stone manse for a response, her stomach knotted. *Lax.* Lady Palmer's favorite word.

"Well, my goodness," her ladyship announced. "Where *is* everyone?"

Lissa took charge, both of her quivering insides and the "laxity." "The Thrings, as I recollect, keep country hours and follow country pursuits. But, never fear, it will soon be right. They are a genuinely nice family."

"Nice?" her ladyship scoffed. "I hardly call this nice."

Max rapped at the front door, smiling over a shoulder at them. "Surely, it will be only a moment," he said.

But no. Several moments passed before there was a response. And then, the door was opened by a bent man with a veil of white hair barely covering his pink pate. " 'Ee must be Missy Pru's friends," he said. "Come in. Come in, if it pleases 'ee. Never had so many at once," he added as they filed in, only to stand in the center hall.

"And Miss Prudence?" Lissa inquired, thinking that Pru

would skip blushingly down the stairs, all apologies for not having heard the coaches.

"Aw," the old man said. "Missy Pru be out. They be ridin' today. Over by Stone Cross way."

"But they are expecting us," Lissa said, hoping he was too deaf to hear Lady Palmer's gasp.

"Oh, aye. They be here for dinner, they say."

"Well," Lissa murmured. Her mind suddenly failed her.

"Yes, well," parroted Max. "No sense in standing here in the hall with our mouths agape."

"My mouth is not agape," Lady Palmer announced.

Max and Lissa pushed on.

That the old house, with its equally aging staff, was unaccustomed to so much company, to so many additional retainers, became more and more clear. As it turned out, the housekeeper was busy with the meal she'd been told to cook, and there wasn't anyone else except the balding man who'd opened the door. It was the stables that were well staffed at Hunt Hall. Those who lived inside "trotted along, making do," the old fellow explained.

Unfortunately, the concept of "making do" was foreign to most of Lissa's companions.

"Lax, lax, lax!" harumphed Lady Palmer.

"Come along, Palmer," Max said easily. "We'll have Bagley help us with the baggage."

"The baggage?" Boysen repeated, as if in need of a definition.

"We have only ourselves, old fellow. If we're to be comfortable, we're the ones to make us so. Your mother, I think, needs a bed."

"Yes," Lissa said. "We'll sort out the rooms while you fetch up the baggage."

There. They had direction, and Max had set the tone. Lissa forced a smile, hoping the others would fall in, equally as cheerfully. Sad hope. Lady Palmer decided on one bedchamber, only to think again. Too drafty, by half. By that time, Lissa was more willing than Aunt Aggie to switch with her, and she and a stone-faced Stowe started settling anew.

The single thing the old butler dragged himself up the stairs to tell them, was that Missy Pru had insisted that His Grace have the room at the end of the passage. The rest of the chambers were theirs to sort out. Always obliging, Max carried his own things to that room. Lissa was left to go to the next floor where she tried to arrange accommodations with Pinseat and Stowe, who had clearly despised one another on sight. Fortunately, Lady Palmer's woman would stay with her ladyship on a trundle. Her ladyship would be sure to need her.

Oddly enough, setting the household to right helped settle Lissa's nerves. Leaving a thoroughly disgruntled Stowe to make do with the scant amenities in the pressing room at Hunt Hall, Lissa went along to the kitchen. There, she threw herself into a process that was the most disorganized of all.

Later, with the help of Max's batman, Lissa saw to it that there were baths. Everyone took up the routine of getting ready for dinner. Aside from Max's encouragement, Bagley, with his paunch and ready smile, assisted Lissa the most. While Max obviously wanted to join them, Lady Palmer's judgment—that it wasn't seemly for His Grace do so—brought even Max to heel. Surely, it wasn't right that His Grace do anything except take his brandy and paper and smelly cigar off to the back parlor. Thoughts of a somewhat bullocked Max made Lissa laugh, genuinely, for the first time in a long while.

At last, everyone waited in the parlor for the return of the Thrings. Dinner was nearly ready, and the party seemed more relaxed except for Lady Palmer. That woman was obviously either asleep or awake, but never relaxed. She believed in neither relaxing herself, nor in allowing others the luxury. She brought her string of judgments and complaints into the parlor, where Max coaxed Aggie to stare out at the view. Boysen retreated to another window, while her ladyship rewrapped her ample figure in her third shawl and took the most likely position in front of the fire.

The strained conversation was interrupted by the return of the family. In they strode, all of them together, all of them florid from their ride outside. Indeed, Lissa had forgotten how handsome the Thrings were. They were tall—taller than she remembered from Pru's come-out season—and as affable as Max.

Lissa fell into Pru's tight hug, and Sir Cornelius went around to shake everyone's hand with a none-too-gentle grasp.

"I hope you settled in well," he said, oblivious to the logistics.

Her ladyship didn't spare her sentiments on that head, and he, together with his son, Finchley, soon escaped with the excuse of dressing for dinner.

Lissa dropped a kiss on Aggie's cheek, and because of Pru's insistence, followed her friend up the stairs to Pru's bedchamber. Pru also wanted to dress for dinner. Shortly after, Lissa fetched Stowe. She saw that Pru could use a little assistance with her rich, brown tresses and sun-colored skin. Although on Pru, the rather unkempt look and especially the color in her face looked very well. Not that she was pretty, but rather attractive. Her glowing health, her confident stride and open smile made it hard not to fall in with her enthusiasm.

Yes, Lissa thought. Pru would do for Max.

"So," Pru said, peering at Lissa through the glass above

her toilette table. She was very direct, despite the dresser who, with pursed lips, arranged her hair. "You must tell me about him."

"You mean, His Grace?"

"Well, who else, silly? He's wonderfully attractive. I've never seen such eyes, such a smile."

Lissa recalled how she and Pru had shared their come-out season with like intimacies. Still, she felt somehow uncomfortable talking about Max at their present ages. And particularly with Stowe listening. "I've been thinking the pair of you looked well together when you were introduced."

"And consider the ways in which we suit."

Truly, it was too soon to be discussing Max so openly, Lissa thought. She and Pru should have time to become reacquainted. Then, Pru and Max could work things out on their own. Pru evidently had no such plans. "When I first heard from you, I thought I'd go dotty. But on seeing him now, I know I will. He's excessively delicious."

Delicious? The word rang oddly in Lissa's mind and caused Stowe's fingers to tremble before going on.

"His Grace," Lissa said, trying to recall them to the proprieties, "is a very nice gentleman."

"To think that he rides as well as anyone, for surely he must when considering his past . . . and then, on seeing that wonderful mount of his. As if that isn't enough, he has a fine leg . . . and those broad shoulders. It's beyond everything!"

While Lissa wanted Pru to appreciate Max, she didn't know how to staunch this enthusiastic flow. She wanted this match, but . . . Well, Pru and she weren't the same people anymore. Pru seemed . . .

"I'm so tired of the gentlemen from around here," Lissa's friend was saying. "Even the men who come for a few days

of shooting or hunting have grown too . . . too familiar.
His Grace—Maxmilian, isn't it?"

"Yes, but . . ."

"Maxmilian will be a treat."

"Pru?" Lissa inquired, with a gentle tone. "Are we clear
on what is going forward here?"

"We could hardly be more clear, Lissa dear. Maxmilian
is out to marry, and to marry quickly. And I, my dear old
friend, am out to marry, as well. I am desperately in need of
a change—of some excitement in my life." Her look was all
too knowing. "Your letters couldn't have come at a more
welcome time."

Lissa was brought to her feet, Pru rising as well. "That
will do, don't you think?" she asked of Lissa. "I'm not one
who's much for fancy toilettes."

Stowe stepped away with a sniff, and Lissa peered at Pru.
She did, indeed, look very well. Once again, Lissa saw the
vitality, the grace of—well, of a healthy animal. Pru had a
confidence that equaled a man's. She'd certainly be able to
match Max tit for tat. Max should like that.

Upon reentering the parlor, Lissa hoped that Max and Pru
might have some time to converse, but everyone else
wanted their dinner. Sir Cornelius and his son, Finchley,
were particularly sharp-set, and the company settled into the
equally unpolished dining room.

And then, it began, exactly as it had in the splendid
dining chamber at Westmane House. Where Lady Palmer
hadn't been the least bit reluctant to belittle the collection of
a very old and illustrious duchy, she openly disparaged
everything Thring.

The dinner was country fare. And although her ladyship
also lived in the country, she didn't see that as an excuse for
so few dishes. Nonetheless, Sir Cornelius commented on
the meal. As did Finchley. The host could sense Lissa's

hand in the repast, and he thanked her heartily. That she was a guest—and that she'd helped in such a matter—didn't appear odd to him in the least.

Max spent the meal talking with Sir Cornelius, while Pru had her own share at that end of the board. Aggie had retreated into heated looks at Lady Palmer days earlier, and continued in that vein. Boysen didn't say much above, "Yes, Mama," and, "Indeed, Mama"—a litany which drove Lissa almost to distraction.

With such a company, nothing could improve, Lissa feared. Not unless Lady Palmer were to take herself off to bed, which she promised to do several times without keeping her promise. When the gentlemen joined the ladies in the parlor, her ladyship sat at the tea tray as if the house were her own. While she pronounced the china charming enough, she couldn't help recollecting Lady Pockington's day set, which was the prettiest blue and white china there could possibly be.

The company turned to cards, and the evening dragged on. Lissa didn't like cards overly much, and when she continued to "woolgather," as her ladyship accused her of doing, she tried to concentrate. What with Boysen being her partner, and he being eager to win, she prayed for the interminable day to end. Max's smile, subdued for the sake of the company, goaded Lissa rather than reassured. Thoroughly exhausted, she retired when Aggie and Lady Palmer did. She left an unabashedly happy Pru with the gentlemen. She'd hoped Pru might come to share a coze with her, but her friend remained behind, sitting in the catbird seat next to Max.

Lissa was too tired to remain and lend countenance to her hostess. After all, both she and Pru were seven and twenty. And, while a certain conduct was expected of them, they were also moving into the years where they could bend some of the rules. At all events, Pru's papa sat on her other side.

"Modern gels," Lady Palmer harumphed outside of Lissa's bedchamber door in lieu of bidding her good night. "Of course we'll leave in the morning."

Since Lissa knew it wasn't their decision to make, she answered as calmly as she could. "It's not mine to decide, my lady."

"Well, I for one, shall go to my bed. I will not get up again until the call to leave."

Lissa prayed this could only be true.

Unbelievably, her ladyship kept her word. The following morning she sent a message, through her son, to those who sat at the breakfast table. The sojourn had proved too much for her, and she simply had to rest. While she hoped to join everyone at dinner, she couldn't make any promises. She knew they would all be thinking of her.

How right she was, Lissa thought. "Do you feel free to leave her?" she asked of her betrothed, when everyone got up from the table.

"Oh, she insists we go ahead and enjoy our day in St. Albans. We've had the outing planned since before leaving London and she, above all people, wouldn't want to spoil our pleasure."

"Well, if you're sure, I'll fetch Aggie and our outer-wear."

He agreed with a nod. "I'll have the carriage brought round."

When Lissa reached the upper corridor, she met Max coming out of his assigned chamber.

"Is it all that much better than the rest?" Lissa asked, alluding to Pru's single instruction for him to stay there.

He smiled. "Not that I can tell. Are you off to St. Albans?"

"Yes."

"The dragon's abed?"

She smiled dryly. "Heaven be praised."

While he chuckled, he seemed more subdued than usual. "I'm off to see the estate. They have some wonderful horses here, and we should be gone all day. Sir Cornelius is as well to grass as we've heard."

"That's why we're here."

"Indeed." He seemed far off. "That's why we're here."

Lissa watched the sway of his broad shoulders as he walked off. While she couldn't expect Max to be happy about his circumstances, she was puzzled. Pru seemed to suit him down to the ground.

As she climbed into the carriage with Aunt Aggie and Boysen, Lissa experienced the familiarity of old routines. Boysen seemed more himself. Gone was the litany of "Yes, Mama." Aggie, too, was cheerful. Her fiery looks to Lissa, their little communications with regard to Lady Palmer and her outrageous observances, abated. Once settled in the vehicle, Aggie even reached over to take Puck on her lap.

For most of the morning the trio wandered about the town of St. Albans. They saw the marketplace, and Boysen explained what he'd heard of the Roman occupation. They had a very nice luncheon in a private room at Ye Old Fighting Cocks Inn. It was held to be the oldest inn in Britain, and while Aggie was reluctant, Boysen enthused over the antiquarian setting. Finally, Boysen and Lissa climbed the old Clock Tower, while Aggie waited with Puck below. The view from the seventy-seven-foot structure, out over the city and its environs, was spectacular. From such a height, Lissa's problems, her deeper worries about what was going forward on the continent, seemed to fade away.

As it turned out, her ladyship deigned to come down for dinner. That meant the time passed much as it had on the night before. The subsequent tea went along equally the same, just as did the evening of cards that followed.

The single surprising difference arose from an unexpected quarter. Max. Max seemed strange to Lissa. He glanced at her often and meaningfully as if he wanted to send her a message. She couldn't read it, though. She wasn't accustomed to reading anything except amusement or reassurance in his amber gaze. Tonight, he was sober. And, most unlikely of all, a trifle . . . angry?

Finally, after failing Boysen at cards yet again, Lissa was allowed to seek her bed.

$\mathcal{L}$ *Chapter Thirteen*

LISSA'S BEDCHAMBER at Hunt Hall was indeed drafty. A long windowseat, upholstered and plump with old cushions, added both charm and tiny currents of leaking air. Still, the view out the window was equally charming, and Lissa, who felt restless and unable to sleep, drifted there, wrapped in a warm coverlet.

She'd often been plagued by restlessness in the past, yet she'd recognized the reason only recently. Being in the country had made her see clearly. She'd always loved Aggie, so being in London with her was fun. But she'd also loved her weeks spent with her maternal grandparents in Oxfordshire. As a youngster, she'd wanted to live in the country. She'd thought she would, in fact. She'd dreamed of living as Judith Battersby did, in a big old house with her children and husband around her. Sadly, she also saw what her life with Boysen would be. He loved town life. To him, living in London was preferable to joining his mother at his country seat. Even Lissa would prefer living in town to a future with that woman.

In the end, Lissa thought she might come to terms with her life. The most unpleasant aspects of her intended's character seemed to emerge only in the presence of his mama. He'd been himself when they'd spent their day together in St. Albans. Once her ladyship returned to her home, she and Boysen would settle in nicely. Along with Aggie, of course. As long as she had Aggie, she had something. And then, she couldn't fault her betrothed there, either. Boysen was invariably considerate, and even generous, with Aggie.

Max, too, would marry and retire to the country. Or so he'd said. He'd close Westmane House and begin again at Bowwood. And he'd do well, she knew he would. No, they'd all settle, if not happily, then nicely. And surely, they'd see each other upon occasion. See each other, that was, if Max didn't push Boysen so far that he took offense; she'd have to handle that situation.

Best of all, Lady Palmer was talking of leaving the Thrings' in her old traveling coach. She longed for her own hearth. Her discussions with Lissa about the wedding had been settled, at least to her own satisfaction. To Lissa's mind, if the woman would only leave, the rest didn't matter.

Sitting in the windowseat, her coverlet wrapped about her, Lissa drifted into a daydream. The moonlight fell in elongated patches across the dusty floorboards, and she thought she heard a nightingale. A log slipped on the fire, and sleep finally tugged at her. Puck certainly slept. His rhythmic snoring sounded from the foot of her bed, as familiar as . . . as soothing as . . .

As Max's voice muttering softly in her ear. Even though he seemed to be complaining about drafts in the window and chill feet, Lissa let herself listen to his voice. His dear voice . . .

But no. A moment later she was dumped unceremoniously on her bed. Max stood above her without his cravat and his boots. His stockinged feet padded soundlessly as he went to the hearth and poked the fire back into life. His vigorous activity sent a shower of sparks up the chimney and a puff of smoke into the room, and Lissa finally knew she was awake. Puck stretched and yawned, wagging his tail as Max walked back in their direction.

"You're really here," Lissa said.

"Now, don't start up on that head." He spoke softly, but his whisper sounded masculine and full of determination. "I need to talk to you."

She straightened against her pillows, her whisper reflecting his. "So, you barge in here? Why am I not surprised?"

"I didn't barge in. I came quietly, and with every consideration for your reputation. Even *you* didn't hear me."

"If you were concerned for my reputation, you wouldn't come in at all."

"Give over, Damalis. I need to talk."

"Is that what those signals and scowls were about this evening?"

"You know it."

By the fire's light, she saw his somber expression. His hair was ruffled, as if he'd been running his fingers through it, and he spoke to her without so much as a hint of his usual levity. "All right—talk. But you must be quick about this. I can't imagine anything worse than you being caught in here."

"Well, I can imagine a lot worse," he bit out, beginning to pace from where she sat in bed to the fire and back. "Just how much do you know of this Pru?"

Lissa collected herself. "I've known Pru . . . well, I told you. My grandparents and Sir Cornelius used to shoot—"

"Yes, yes," Max said, shortly. "You were girlhood friends and you shared your bows. But since then. What do you know of her?"

"Not much. Since my grandparents died, I've lived in

London. Pru has lived here at Hunt Hall. A few times a year we correspond, but she doesn't like to write. I must admit I was somewhat surprised when I saw her again. I didn't recollect her being so tall."

"Tall? Tall? What does tall . . . ?" Max's finger stabbed at the air in the general direction of the door. "That woman is out to get me."

Lissa had visions of knives and ropes. "What?" she said, horrified.

"She's out to have me, I tell you."

"You mean, to marry you?"

"Yes. And *whatever* else in the meanwhile."

"But I thought that's what you wanted."

"Oh, no!" In this instance his voice rasped in a hoarse whisper. He was every inch the colonel. "Not like this. It's *I* who makes this decision. It's *I* who makes the advance."

"Max, pray, keep your voice down."

"Beg pardon," he murmured.

"Perhaps, you'd better try to explain."

He began to pace again, his fingers in fact running his hair. "This . . . this female has made no secret of her intentions. Not even in front of her father and brother, deuce it all."

"But I thought your intentions match her evident intentions."

He turned all starch. "Pray, hear me out."

Lissa sat back, quietly watching him.

"From the moment I laid eyes on her, I knew what she was about. I've been on the other end of many a bold glance and, by and large, such nonsense doesn't bother me. But this . . . this is beyond belief. She's supposed to be a lady."

"She is a lady. It's just that she's been raised a little

differently than most of the ladies you've met in town. I thought you'd find her refreshing."

"*Refreshing?* Is it *refreshing* to have someone stalking you like prey? Last night—but no, you're too much of a lady to hear."

Lissa felt insulted. Max usually told her everything. "You had best tell me and be quick about it."

His amber eyes studied her. But then, he began, albeit reluctantly. "Every chance she has, she . . . she rubs against me like some deuced cat. Last night, under the card table, she touched my ankle with the toe of her shoe. When I looked at her, she . . . well, thunderation, she all but winked at me, what with those fluttering lashes."

Lissa surprised them both by chuckling. Truly, she thought she should be shocked. Pru was her friend, and she was supposed to be a lady. But Max's reaction, when considering the life he'd lead . . . well, it struck her as comical.

"Damnation, Damalis! This is not a laughing matter."

"No, Max." She tried to contain herself. "This is not a laughing matter. I'm sure it's merely the . . . hour." Still, another giggle escaped. He stared at her, all the harder. "Max," she pleaded, collecting herself by holding her eyes to his level, amber gaze. "What with your years and experience, I'm sure you know how to handle this. When you and Pru are married, you will—"

"Married? Married? Oh, no. I'll not marry her. I'd never know whose ankle she might be nudging under what table. Marriage is out of the question."

"Well, that's yours to decide. We'll simply leave here tomorrow, and no one will be the worse for the experience. I understand perfectly. And I'm sure you'll know what to say to Sir Cornelius. The pair of you have—"

"I'm not worried about leaving tomorrow."

"Then, what is it?"

"It's tonight, deuce it."

He was more angry now than when he'd started. Lissa had thought they'd talked it out. "I don't understand."

"Think about this, my girl. The room, remember? The only room that was strictly allotted. My room. It has no lock."

Lissa gasped. "Max! Surely, you aren't suggesting—"

"No, I'm not suggesting. I'm telling you as plain as day. That female is out to compromise me."

"Max!"

"She's decided that, one way *or another*, she'll have herself a husband."

Lissa could see he believed his words. As ludicrous as it sounded, he was convinced.

"Since the lock is broken," she said, "could you not somehow barricade the door to keep . . . well, you know what I'm saying."

From his expression, he'd obviously thought of this. "Except for my bed, which would take three or four of us to move, there isn't a stick of furniture in that chamber that could serve such a purpose. And then, what if there's a secret door I haven't been able to discover? As you can well imagine, I've rapped at every square inch of the paneling. Not knowing of some hidden access worries me the most."

"So," Lissa said, sighing, but still wanting to help. And especially wanting to get Max out of her room. "What else is there to do?"

"I simply need some place to run to ground. . . ."

"Yes, I see that."

"I'm staying in here."

"Well, I never. You're saying you'd rather compromise me!"

"Gad, no. But where else can I go?"

"Well, you'll have to think of someplace else."

"I've been trying to. But I can't. Can you? Go on. Suggest someplace where I can sleep without raising a ruckus. Someplace where I won't leave myself open to that . . . that . . . hussy."

Lissa thought she might chuckle again. This was all so impossibly silly. A country mouse had a lion in retreat. Even so, Max seemed earnest. Additionally she couldn't think of a single place for him to spend the rest of the night, not without there being some question, either tonight or in the morning.

"Oh, botheration," she finally said. "On the windowseat, I suppose. But I warn you, Max, you had better be out of here before anyone else is up in the morning. And that includes the servants."

Just that quickly, his disposition turned sunny. "I'll be eternally grateful, my girl. And don't worry, I sleep light. I'll leave before the first cock's crow."

Lissa could hardly believe what was happening, but Max padded over to the windowseat as naturally as if he slept there every night. Of course, there were no covers, nor even a really nice pillow. "Max," she called to him. "I have two covers—"

"No, no," he said, accommodating his large frame to the narrow seat. "I'm fine. I've slept in worse."

Pushing a cushion under his head, his arms crossed and his large stockinged feet hanging over the edge, he closed his eyes. Lissa, who had never been able to sleep without the conditions being precisely right, couldn't imagine he'd drift off so quickly. Lying down herself, she stared at the ceiling. As impossible as it seemed, Max was actually sleeping in her room. It was unheard of. She must be unbalanced.

Later still, and wide awake, Lissa looked to the windowseat again. Max remained exactly as he'd lain down, his eyes shut but surely not asleep. She thought about the drafts that swirled, however faintly, about the embrasure. Max seemed so uncomfortable. He might even catch cold.

Gingerly, she got up from her bed. She still wore her wrapper over her gown. Even so, she felt . . . well, all the things any exposed lady would feel. A man slept in her room. Then again, this was Max, and that knowledge emboldened her. She cared for him. No, she loved him, and he must be freezing.

Creeping up on him, her second cover spread wide, she carefully laid it across him, up to his chin. No sooner had it touched him, than his hand swept out from beneath where the cover had settled, capturing her wrist.

"I . . . I thought you might be cold," she stammered.

"I'm sorry. As I told you, I sleep light."

She looked at where his hand still grasped her wrist, then into his eyes. That golden gaze returned her stare. "Come here," he whispered, tugging at her.

"No, I . . . I . . ."

"Come here," he said, even more softly.

His gaze locked to hers. She couldn't look away. Letting go of her wrist, he grasped the thick braid that swung at her shoulder. He tugged at it, and she sank to a knee. Her face dropped closer to his.

"Kiss me, Damalis."

Her heart pounded. His amber stare sapped her resistance. His honeyed voice, she loved so well.

"Please," he coaxed. "Forget you are engaged and that I am to marry. For this one time, forget and kiss me."

Lissa knew it was wrong, and yet she . . . she couldn't look away. Her head drifted nearer to where he waited, as quiet as the moonlight glowing about them. His eyes riveted to hers, he put the fragrant rope of her hair to his lips.

"Now, your mouth on mine," he said, letting the braid swing free.

Lissa's lips touched Max's. The contact was as sweet as his honeyed eyes, as warm as his breath. His hand smoothed along her nape, and he deepened what she'd started. His groan spoke of his pleasure. It ignited something in her that slept.

And then, before Lissa could think what had happened, Max was on his feet. It was his turn to stare at her. He did so, in fact, as he backed toward the door. "I . . . I can't sleep in here," he said, as if he'd been mad to consider it.

"But . . . but, what did I . . . ? I mean, what . . . ?"

Finally aroused, Puck tipped his head, his pop-eyes staring first at Lissa and then at Max. But Max continued to back toward the door, his hand groping behind him for the handle. "Gad, I'm sorry, but 'fore George, Damalis, I can't stay."

"But where will you sleep?"

"I don't know. I'll find an inn."

"An inn? But you'll have to call a stablelad to saddle Pegasus."

"The gazebo, then. There's a gazebo outside the window."

"What?" She tracked him to the door where he stood staring at her with that same odd expression about his eyes. "Max, what is it? You look as if you've been struck."

"Oh, my God, my girl. That's exactly it. I have been struck. And by the not-so-proverbial barge pole."

"But whatever do you mean? You must have been dreaming, and . . ."

But he was opening the door, looking down the hall. "Believe me, my love," he said over his shoulder. "I cannot stay."

Then, he was gone. Simply gone.

Lissa stumbled back to bed, where Puck snuggled his head to his paws. She knew she'd never sleep. She was doubly amazed, in fact, when she awoke, sunlight streaming across the windowseat. Peering at the clock, she saw she was already behind schedule. Thoughts of Max pressed in on her. It was imperative they leave Hunt Hall as planned. Then, as if everything went against her, Stowe appeared at the ring of her bell, only to tell her she could hardly hold up her head. Indeed, the woman, who had the constitution of a horse, looked white.

A few more words disclosed the dresser's distaste for Boysen's man. She'd been forced to share the pressing room with him yet again this morning. Her dislike had grown so intense that she felt ill.

Lissa assured the woman they would be leaving shortly. In the meanwhile, she encouraged her to rest while she could. Unfortunately, the dresser's departure complicated Lissa's further preparations. They also left her with no opportunity to think about Max. She couldn't imagine where he'd spent the night. Nor even why he'd left the way he had.

The most obvious suggestion—that her kiss had revolted him somehow—nearly revolted her. No. She would not think about that kiss until she had both the peace and cogency to sort it through.

Arriving in the dining room even more behind time, Lissa was surprised to find Lady Palmer getting up from the table along with the rest. "I'm sorry, I'm late," Lissa said, avoiding Max's eyes.

He seemed, however, to be evading her altogether.

"Lissa," Boysen said, coming over to lean from behind and speak into her ear.

"Yes?"

"Since you are having only hot chocolate, would you

please step outside onto the terrace for a moment? After you've finished, of course."

Since the terrace stretched behind the house, exactly beyond the glass in the dining room doors, Lissa said she'd join him in a minute. The possibility that he'd found out about Max being in her bedchamber pounded color into her cheeks and guilt into her breast. As calmly as she could, she finished her hot chocolate. The others were going about their last minute preparations for leaving. Everything seemed amicable enough, and she thought Max must have smoothed the situation with every discretion.

Still, she avoided his eyes. Even when he hovered about the table where she drank her chocolate. Finally, she went out the glass-paned doors to join Boysen.

"Lissa, my dear," Lord Palmer said, his features aligned in distaste.

Her heart had never beat so hard. "Yes, Boysen?"

"Have you any idea as to how your hair looks?"

Relief began to nudge at her. "Yes. I realize it's untidy. And my gown, too. You see, Stowe is feeling unwell, and I had to make do for myself."

"You should have called for Mama's woman."

"I disliked the idea of disturbing them. What with the rush this morning—"

Still, he remained, stubbornly standing over where she'd ended up sitting on a very cold stone bench. Boysen was a stickler for appearances. "Your hair, Lissa . . . Well, we had best set it straight between us now. Your hair, in particular, is very unladylike. It tends—and don't take me amiss in this—but you must admit that it tends to a naturalness which can approach the unseemly. A woman's hair, you know, is—as my mother says—the very work of the devil. It is designed for the entrapment of men. It is important, then, that you keep a particular guard on yours, which is overly abundant. I don't mean to read you a lecture, but . . ."

But he did read her a lecture, there on the unkempt terrace at Hunt Hall. Needless to say, it embarrassed Lissa. The sunlight streaming down, catching in the curls that even now escaped despite her meager efforts, verified every word he said. And Lissa resented most of it. He was to be her husband, and he had his rights to tell her what he thought. But that he thought she should be corrected much like a child, rankled.

Worse yet, Lissa caught sight of Max, nudging at the glass door that led into the dining room. Although she held her head high, she couldn't help her now acute embarrassment, both for herself and for Boysen.

It was, however, when she saw Max flush, when she saw his fists clench, that her heart began to race again. She worried crazily that he might knock Boysen down. Max looked that angry. Her eyes pleaded with his strange, amber stare. She silently begged him to let it pass. If there were to be a rift, Boysen would never allow her to see Max again.

At last, he turned aside. Boysen finished just as Max closed the door behind his broad-shouldered figure. Lissa released a breath, hoping to get to her feet as gracefully as she could. She couldn't leave Hunt Hall quickly enough, now.

Later, the sight of Lady Palmer's coach separating itself from the cavalcade at the first crossroads seemed to be the best outcome of the whole trip.

Chapter Fourteen

LADY AGATHA WESTMANE waited for Max in the painted parlor where late morning sunlight shafted in. Aggie hadn't seen Max since the previous week, when they'd left the Thrings. What a disaster that visit had been, she thought. Even so, Max had obviously absolved them well. They'd left, not so much under a cloud, as with a cheery fare-thee-well from a lone Sir Cornelius.

While she didn't know what Max would do next, she suspected he'd continue their campaign for finding a duchess. A *suitable* duchess. She just thought it unusual that Lissa hadn't been included in his hastily scrawled request for a meeting. If anything, that pair was avoiding one another like the plague.

Absently stroking Puck's silky head, for the aging Pekingese was more and more in her company, Aggie thought again about the ladies she might suggest to Max. It had reached the first of June, and they were running out of both time and prospects. Well, any prospects she could recommend with a good conscience and whole heart.

Max then entered the antique parlor. Aggie smiled, while Puck got up to wag his tail and accept Max's quick pat.

"How are you, old fellow? And you, Aggie dear, how do you go on?"

Looking into Max's face, Aggie was somewhat surprised. He appeared somehow changed—less easy, more resolute. Dark smudges marked his eyes. "What is it, Max?" she asked.

"Nothing to worry about," he replied, petting Puck's head.

Even more surprisingly, he turned away, walking stiffly to a window. There he peered out at the distant traffic on Piccadilly. "I've come a cropper, Aggie," he finally said.

When she didn't reply—didn't know how to reply—he plunged ahead. "I've never been in love before. And I'm sure I need not name the lady."

Aggie was stunned. What she'd hoped . . .

But his gaze focused beyond the drive. "I had a friend once. A fellow officer. This was under Wellesley, then, at Vimeiro. In any case, this fellow received word—actually, little more than gossip. His sweetheart, here in London, was having an affair with someone else. The fellow, er, my friend, put a pistol to his head and shot himself. At the time, I couldn't understand such an act. But now . . . well, I'm not saying I'm about to take up my pistol, but . . ."

Aggie's voice sounded thick. "Go to her. Tell her. Engagements can be broken."

Putting his hands behind his back, he locked them there. "I have nothing to offer her, Aggie. And I need to watch out for us all. As soon as you and she are safely off to Palmer House, I'm closing up here. I want to be shot of London now. I plan to throw myself into restoring Bowwood. There will be nothing in Derbyshire but hard work and sacrifice. Even if I do marry, I plan to set up a little place here for a wife. No one will want to share what's ahead of me."

"But, Max, don't you think that's for Lissa to decide?"

"No," he said stoutly. "It's mine to decide."

Aggie could see his resolution. She also saw his pain.

She could only think to regroup, to help him as she could.
She pushed at her weighty coif. "So, you mean to make one
more try at finding a duchess?"

"Aye."

"I have a few thoughts—"

"No. No one with any expectations of a nearly traditional
union. I can't, in good conscience, marry a woman knowing
I have no heart to share. Nor will that ever be possible.
What I need now is a different sort of lady. One who needs
a bargain as much as I do. You mentioned one time, when
we first began discussing possible matches, a Lady Baird."

"Barbara Baird?" she repeated, unbelieving. "But,
Max—"

"Pray, Aggie, tell me about her. And don't spare our
blushes."

Goodness, but she didn't want to. Still, if she could read
anything in the set of Max's broad shoulders, it was
resolution. "Well, she's a beautiful lady. Although her
father ruined them with gambling, she comes from a good
family. She married very young; another gentleman of good
standing, one who was extraordinarily wealthy. An older
gentleman, with no family . . ." Aggie could sense that
Max knew where she was leading. "After he died and she
was left with his fortune, she married again."

"To the same sort of man, no doubt."

Aggie nodded. "The elderly Lord Baird. None of that
would have excluded her from society. But there have been
rumors, particularly since before Baird died. Rumors of—"

"Of other *younger* gentlemen."

"Yes. So, you see you can't—"

"Oh, but I can. And I will. At least, I'll try."

"But Max, you'll never be accepted. Not by the sticklers.
Those on the fringe will always recognize a duke, but even
a duke with such a wife—"

Finally, he turned to smile at her. "I'll not ask you to put her in my way."

"As if I could," she replied, somewhat briskly. "I'm not acquainted with her. Few are. And I especially don't like this."

"I know. I take full responsibility. You've warned me."

Aggie couldn't resist that brief, easy look about him. He simply had a way, and her defenses, her effort to stand proof, faded into thoughts for some other—*any* other—possibility. "If only we could uncover Mad Jack's treasure," she murmured.

He chuckled, coming to drop a kiss on her brow. "I think I hear Mad Jack laughing at us even now, Aggie dear."

"Oh, Max. Surely—"

"Now, now. None of that." He paused at the door. "Not a word of this. I know I can rely on you."

Although she'd been told differently, Lissa felt as if she looked a bit off color. She and Stowe had spent some time over her toilette, and indeed, when considering her mode of dress here of late, her gown was very dashing. While the white figured satin, trimmed with white *crêpe* and chenille, wasn't all that unusual, the cut of the gown was very complimentary to her shoulders and upper bosom.

Still, all she wanted was to take a book to her bed. She certainly didn't want to remain at the Rodney ball. She didn't want to smile, and converse . . . to listen to Boysen. He stood beside her—at least, physically if not mentally attentive.

The ballroom was hot and crowded. The Rodneys had all sorts of acquaintances, ranging the many subtle levels of *tonnish* company. Indeed, she could be sure their every friend had packed into this one room.

Boysen sniffled into his handkerchief before speaking into her ear. "Blaycock told me he's to be here tonight."

"Who's to be here?"

"Your . . . His Grace."

Though her stomach fluttered, Lissa couldn't help grasping at this bit of information. She hadn't even glimpsed Max in the two weeks since their return from the Thrings' during the third week in May. Of course, she'd heard as much about him as anyone else had.

London had been set on its ear. In the past week or so, he'd taken up with Barbara Baird, and nothing could have fascinated The Fashionables more. While everyone knew he needed to marry, none would have thought that someone— even someone so new on the Town—would have taken such a desperate step. And now they were to be here at the Rodney ball. As much as Lissa longed to see Max, she couldn't face the certain reaction.

"Of course," Boysen said, to draw her attentions to his unusually anxious expression, "he would choose tonight."

"Tonight?" she inquired without thinking.

Boysen's pale brows knotted in disbelief. His voice was a low hiss. "Why, Lissa, yes! Tonight! You may not think much of the Palmer Frond, but you know I've been waiting weeks to spring my knot on the *monde*."

"I beg your pardon, Boysen. I didn't mean . . . I've been so . . ."

"Yes. What is amiss with you, Lissa? You haven't been the same since our return from the Thrings'."

Lissa's best hope was to change the subject. "Pray, forgive me. Forgive me and tell me what Mr. Brummell said."

"But I told you."

"I know." Lissa struck open her fan in front of her face. Maybe some air would calm her. "Perhaps if you repeat what he said, we'll find something in it that we didn't notice before."

"Well," Boysen said, making an attempt at recovering some of his usual aplomb, "I—like I said—went straight up to him. We've only spoken a few times over any number of years, but he seemed to recognize me. His eyes—he has the sharpest eyes, you know—well, they focused immediately on my neckcloth. I wished him a good evening, and he returned the favor. Oh," Boysen said, diverted by his recollection, "he does dress wonderfully well. Of course, I prefer something aside from a blue coat once in a while, but . . . Where was I?"

"You said good evening to him, and he looked at your neckcloth."

"Yes. And then, he said, 'How very interesting.' "

" 'How very interesting,' " Lissa repeated, musingly. "He said nothing else?"

"Not a word. We bowed and parted, and . . . well, there was not another word."

The pair stood for a moment in silence.

"Oh, Lissa," Boysen said, all in a rush. "If he would only take it up, the Palmer Frond would be made."

A pink flush colored Boysen's cheeks. Lissa reached down inside of herself and tried—tried very hard—to empathize, to encourage him, to . . .

But she couldn't. In all their hours together, she'd never felt more indifferent to this man. Not that she would cry off. She was even more desperate to marry him. She was even more convinced it was right she did so. She knew Boysen's feelings paralleled hers. They were as pale as his coloring, as pale as his smile, as pale as her own feelings. Their marriage would be suitable. They'd go along comfortably. She would make Boysen happy and hope to find a content- ment for herself. They had, in fact, been rubbing along very well since his mother had returned to the country. Very well, until tonight. Somehow she had to share in Boysen's concern. She had to support his wishes for his sartorial invention. She had to face Max and appear as if she had no other wishes than these.

Boysen's voice interrupted her thoughts. "How would you interpret the phrase, 'very interesting'?"

"Well, how did he say it?"

"Crisply. But then, he has unusual ways of saying one thing and meaning another. He's excessively clever, you know."

"Yes, I've heard." Lissa didn't like Brummell, at least, not what she knew of him. For all her Town bronze, she'd given Mr. Brummell a wide birth. "I suppose only time will tell," she finally said. "You'll simply have to wait and see how many men adopt the tie."

"Alas, it isn't an easy one to do. Not that most fellows don't like a challenge. It's more that the initial pleatings are very important. I can't tell you how many cloths Pinseat pressed and ruined before we hit on this one."

Lissa forced herself to listen. Still, her mind wandered. She used her fan, but she remained heated. She sensed the beginnings of a headache and couldn't seem to keep her eyes from the door. Max was coming tonight. She'd see the man she loved, again. She knew those occasions were numbered.

And then, he was there. Tall and confident. Lissa's eyes, however, fixed on Barbara Baird. "Glittering" was the first word to come to her mind. The twice-widowed woman was wealthy, and her diamonds proclaimed this fact. The next word to present itself was, of course, beautiful. Lady Baird was an extraordinary beauty, with guinea-gold hair and milk-white skin. The latter was amply displayed for all to see above the deep cut of her décolletage. Lissa felt sick.

Even so, she watched. She couldn't restrain herself. Lord Rodney, an old military man and an even older roué, went to clap Max on the back. If his lordship hadn't rushed the new arrival off to the cardroom, Lissa didn't know what would have gone forward after that. As to Lady Baird, she had enough friends, particularly among the gentlemen, to make her progress through the crowd a comfortable one. She even danced a set. And then, another.

Lissa danced as well. She sat on a chair next to Aggie's. She chatted with friends. But her mind wasn't there. And her head pounded terribly.

Nearly two hours later, Boysen spoke scathingly. "He's in the cardroom. He's playing for high stakes and winning. They're saying he's heartless in his play. Evidently, he's making free use of his brandy flask. That will raise even more talk. While I've always thought him too easy, I would never have believed him a loose fish. As Mama would say, old habits die hard."

Lissa couldn't believe her ears. This didn't sound like the Max she knew. She wanted to defend him. Collecting her accessories as calmly as she could, she excused herself and walked toward the withdrawing room. She hoped to find a moment of peace—a moment in which to let her heart and head stop beating. She especially needed time away from the heat and candles of the ballroom.

Outside, there was a circle of the season's debs in a controlled but nonetheless excited group. Vaguely she overheard the news that Lady Daphne and Simon Tuttle were to be married.

Smiling and partially recovered, Lissa went along the passageway. The Rodney manse was marked with "things Egyptian," and she swept past a hideous tripod plant stand, supported by ibises with down-curved bills, with a slight sniff. Lissa, who was accustomed to every sort of carved

face and combination of parts in furniture design, neverthe-
less found the Egyptian mode distasteful. Going on, she
assured herself she'd steal only a moment away. Merely
enough time to cool her heated forehead.

Passing several anterooms, all of them lighted and
welcoming, she finally paused. The one she chose, simply
because it was the farthest along the corridor, had a cheerful
fire and was, once again, accented in the Egyptian style.
Avoiding the uncomfortable looking crocodile couch, a
mere curving piece of green and gilt wood with grotesque
feet, she moved to a window embrasure. Glad for the shadows
and quiet, she stared out on the June night. June fifteenth. June
fifteenth had arrived, and the wager she'd made with Max had
set his limit for marrying to the eighteenth. She wondered if
he'd make it. She wondered if he recollected the wager.
Perhaps he had forgotten.

It was just as well. How she'd ever had the nerve to
wager with him, she still hadn't thought. That night in
the library, when she'd found him asleep in the chair,
remained a magical memory. As did all her times with him.
She'd always remember every moment. She'd use those
treasured moments in the hard days ahead.

Feeling somewhat restored, Lissa turned from the velvet
darkness only to see Max. He stood in the doorway, moving
neither in nor out. Their eyes met.

"I didn't see you," she said.

"I've been here for a minute," he admitted. "But I didn't
want to frighten you. And then, it was a pleasure to look."

Lissa wanted to smile, to turn his compliment away just
as she usually did. But this man wasn't Max. This man was
a stranger. His eyes didn't shine clear like sherry. They were
flat, rather like the gold color of an old and patinated coin.

Much to her surprise and secret delight, he moved into

the room. She'd expected he would leave. As she probably should.

"I had come to blow a cloud," he said.

Lissa thought he already smelled heavily of cigarillos and brandy, but he didn't appear in his cups.

"Don't let me keep you from enjoying your tobacco."

"Are you sure?" he asked. "But then, you're a different person from when we first met. I would imagine that the Damalis I've come to know wouldn't deny me my least pleasure."

The words refused to skip lightly between them, as they would have in the past. They hung, weighted by Max's emphasis on the word *pleasure*. Perhaps, he'd imbibed too much, after all. Perhaps she should leave.

But he was moving to the fire, bending with a faggot in hand to light the cigarillo he took from a pocket. Lissa felt rooted to the spot. She couldn't take her eyes from this new—yes, this *dangerous* Max.

"I just heard some good news," she said, a little nervously.

He pivoted from the fire, puffing at his cigarillo to get it going. "Oh? I could use some good news."

"I've heard that Daphne and Simon are to be married. An announcement will be made at Christmas, and the wedding will follow next spring."

"Old Huntley's making 'em wait, is he?"

"That was the original objection against the match. That Simon is too young."

"Simon's a right 'un, though," Max insisted. He drew more deeply, the end of the tobacco embering with the flow of his breath. "Thimon, eh?" he said more softly, more himself. "Good for him."

A moment passed. Lissa enjoyed it. And then, Max peered at her suddenly, disquieting her. "Are you all right?"

"I was merely taking a moment. The ballroom is hot tonight. I have a bit of a headache."

Abruptly, Max turned and tossed his cigarillo onto the fire. "You should have told me. I wouldn't have lit the thing."

"But it doesn't bother me."

"Just as well."

"And you?" Lissa managed. "How are you?"

He stared at her. Finally, he let down the tightness in his shoulders. "I'm all right. I guess you've seen my latest marital objective?" he asked.

"Max." She continued hesitant. "Surely, you aren't considering that silly wager."

"What wager? Oh. No."

"You must not. We can all stay in London for a while. There are other nice ladies—"

"No, no. I want to get this over with—now. Lady Baird is merely one last try. If she doesn't . . . well, I'll go to Bowwood one way or another. That much I'm determined on." His voice and face were a blank facade again. "Are you as shocked as everyone else?"

She didn't know what to say, but he went on in any case. "Well, everyone has a right to be shocked. Lady Baird is a shocking lady."

He sounded disgusted, but once again, Lissa didn't reply. In this instance, they were interrupted. Boysen entered the room, his pale eyes unusually intractable as they ran first to Lissa and then to Max.

"I've been looking for you," he said to her.

"I'm quite all right," she replied.

Boysen straightened. "This isn't the thing, you know. And I'm most tired of it. Finding the pair of you closeted together."

"You have a fine way of greeting a fellow," Max said. "And how very solicitous you are of your intended."

"I fail to see why I should be solicitous."

"Your affianced bride has the megrim."

"I didn't know."

Max's eyes glittered. Lissa recalled the morning on the terrace at the Thrings'. His eyes had glittered just so on that occasion, as well.

"Please," she said, moving to Boysen's stubborn figure. She had the impression that Max was like a chained bear whose chain had a weak link. "I'm feeling more the thing now. We can go and leave His Grace to his tobacco."

"Very well," Boysen said, stuck in place. "I will have one word, however. If you please, Westmane. I've never approved of the light manner in which you treat my fiancée. But I haven't felt I had a right to say anything. Or a true need to—not until this last week." As they all knew, his allusion was to Barbara Baird. Still, he left her name unspoken as he went ahead, stiff as a ramrod. "Under your present circumstances, and considering the company you've chosen to keep, I hope to never find Lissa in a situation like this again."

"But Boysen," Lissa said, all conciliation, "we merely ran across one another."

"It makes no difference. I expect Westmane to leave a room when you enter it. It's only right."

Max spoke, his voice and his eyes deceptively controlled. "Damalis lives with me. She's my family. We are bound to run across one another, and I will not embarrass either of us with such unmitigated nonsense. I'll see to it that she doesn't have to encounter Lady Baird, but I will not otherwise insult her good sense."

The occurrence Lissa had always dreaded looked about to happen. Boysen could easily decide to never allow her to see Max again. And, once they were married, he could enforce that dictum. Her heart pounding, she pleaded with Max without saying a word.

"Look, Palmer. I have as much respect for Damalis as you do. I—"

"You don't. You cannot. I wouldn't find you with her like this if you did."

The nightmare deepened. "It isn't as if you found Damalis in my arms, for God's sake. We were merely conversing."

"That you can even make such a suggestion demonstrates my point."

Max exploded into a controlled but nonetheless definite reply. "The day you walk in on us and find her in my arms is the day you can cry compromise. But your mistrust is so far off the mark as to make you appear the one with improper thoughts. God's bones. Damalis belongs to you. I'm fully aware of that fact, while you seem to take damned too little note."

"You will watch your language, sirrah."

"I'll damn well say this, Palmer. If Damalis were mine, you would've found exactly what you thought to find. You wouldn't have to make it up out of whole cloth. As it is, you're insulting us both with your suspicions. Damalis deserves better than your mistrust. And especially your lectures. If she were mine . . . if she were mine," he said, his voice stretching to a soft but tense crescendo.

But no. His eyes, his dangerous eyes, glowed like molten gold into Lissa's shocked stare. Without another word, he left, striding from the room in his best military bearing.

Shortly thereafter, when Lissa and Boysen returned to the ballroom—as if nothing had happened—the place ran rife with conjecture. It seemed the new duke had made a spectacular exit. He'd come into the ballroom with Lady

Baird's wrap flung over his arm, his own evening cape swirling around him like a dark cloud.

He'd simply grabbed her by the wrist and led her off. He hadn't even expressed his gratitude to his hostess. Worse, the front door had slammed behind him before the surprised footman had been able to prevent it, reverberating all the way to the ballroom. No one had the slightest idea as to what had set him off.

♋ Chapter Fifteen

As if Lissa didn't have enough to concern her, the day after the Rodney ball, rumors about Bonaparte's collection of troops along the Sambre began to spread. Some 200,000 men it was said. Surely the old tyrant would soon be in Brussels where Wellington had been in command of the Allied forces since April.

Lissa could think only of Max. She realized he had to be worried about his comrades across the channel, and she felt a desperate need to see him. She didn't know what she'd say, or even if she could comfort him, but she wanted to see him.

Glimpsing a London gentleman in the streets—freshly rigged out in a uniform that supposedly tied him somehow to the events that they all feared were going forward in Belgium—caused her heart to start. A dash to the mews to check that Pegasus was still there lent her a moment's relief. Seeing the great white remuda, munching on his hay, meant that Max remained in London, if not at Westmane House. Time and again, Lissa wondered where he could be. He was either at the Guards' Club, which had a room in a coffee house at the bottom of St. James's Street, opposite Lock's, or, *oh lud*, he was with Barbara Baird.

Finally, on the twenty-second of June, Lissa awoke to a

definite change in the air. Church bells had begun to peel, sounding from one steeple, to one tower, to one spire, to the next. London was rich in churches, and there were many bells. Shouts were heard, both within the house and without. Extra editions were hawked in the streets. Surely, it had to be over. But where was Max? A week had passed since she'd seen him at the Rodney ball.

At tea time, Boysen arrived with the news—an exact recounting of what she'd been reading in the papers. On June eighteenth, on the day that had been Max's mother's birthday, on the day that had been touch and go on the continent until dusk, the Old Guard carried out a superb fighting retreat, but lost it all. It was over. At least, for now. Boney had fled to Paris.

"Indeed," Boysen said, a picture of delight in the painted parlor, where Aggie and Lissa hung on his every word. "The Honorable H. Bennet was sitting in Brooks's Club with Earl Grey and Sir Robert Wilson. Wilson was reading a letter which spoke of how the English were defiling out of Brussels by the Antwerp gate. The gentlemen were horribly discomfited, when they heard shouts in the street. Of course, everyone went to the window, and Bennet saw the very chaise and Eagles."

"Chaise and Eagles?" Aggie inquired.

Boysen's flush at recounting the news colored his cheeks. "Yes, Lady Westmane. Major the Honorable Henry Percy, one of Wellington's staff, traveled straight from the battlefield of Waterloo to announce the victory to the Regent. Percy found His Highness at Mrs. Boehm's party in St. James's Square. 'Tis said that Mrs. Boehm was annoyed with the battle of Waterloo, as it spoilt her party. And of course, the disruption must have been excessively upsetting for the hostess. What with the major in his travel dirt, and all. But then, think of it. The Regent actually knighted the officer who laid the insignia of the *Grande Armée* at his feet."

"My stars," Aggie said, her sense of adventure shining in her eyes, "what a tale."

Boysen continued to preen, as if it were all his doing—as if he'd even witnessed the event. "Indeed, what a sight it was, my lady. Henry Percy, rushing through the streets of London in his carriage, defeated French Eagles and battle standards sticking through its windows. I'm certain it was well worth the travel dirt to deliver such news."

But Lissa was now barely diverted by Boysen's pale comparisons on the matter. *Travel dirt, indeed.*

Where was Max?

That night, Lissa and Boysen and Aggie were supposed to attend a party in St. James, the very site of last evening's triumph. Still, Lissa knew the do at the Truewoods' wouldn't be anything elaborate. She wished she didn't have to go. She could hardly sit still, despite the news of victory and the drunken celebration in the streets. Even so, she knew it would be easier to go than not to go. The Truewoods were particular friends of Boysen's, and to cry off would cause a stir.

Really, Lissa didn't know why she didn't want to go. Mr. and Mrs. Geoffrey Truewood were a newly married couple of their own age. Lissa thought she recollected Max mentioning Geoffrey as a fellow officer in the Peninsular Campaign who'd sold out.

Naturally, that decided it. She would go to the Truewoods'. As usual, Stowe threw herself wholeheartedly into both Lissa's coif and costume. A simple white muslin gown, with white satin trim, was topped by an Indian ruby mantle edged with gold.

But alas, disappointment awaited Lissa at the Truewoods'. While there were cards and the expected conversation, Max didn't number among the guests.

Much later, when she was on the verge of asking Boysen if they could leave, Max was surprisingly admitted to the large, second-story chambers. By then, the party had separated into those who continued to play cards, and those who sat here and there in conversation. Since the night was warm the doors onto the balcony were thrown open, and Lissa was just stepping back into the room when he was welcomed in. Exactly as she thought, he and Geoffrey Truewood fell into an immediate conversation concerning the recent occurrences. Finally, Max apologized for his late arrival, and Clare Truewood insisted he come in and greet the rest of her guests.

Later, Max moved around to Lissa. Since she'd waited for days to see him, her eyes drank in his appearance greedily.

"I've been so worried about you," she said, as they stepped somewhat aside, nearer to the open balcony doors.

"I've been mostly at the Guards' Club. I wouldn't have come tonight, except I ran into old Geoff earlier in the day and he insisted."

Lissa saw the lines about Max's eyes and in his brow. He looked more subdued, almost his old self. She could tell he was tired, but there was something else about him. Something said that the more dangerous Max of the Rodney ball had gone—gone to leave her dear, familiar, Max in control.

"I'm sorry if I've worried you and Aggie," he said. "But I wasn't fit for much except male company. As you can see, I've cut my ties with Lady Baird." This latter he pronounced more softly, his amber eyes running the round of the guests. "Let's step out on the balcony, shall we? I think we should have a few words."

The old manse looked out over the heart of Town, over

St. James's Square. The excitement of the day had mellowed into a warm jubilation. People still called in the street below, and torches made patches of moving, yellowed light. Across the park, the occasional silver streak and thudding retort announced a firework.

"It's been a hard won thing, you see," Max finally said. "All the while this other business was going on, I've been battling with myself. We won't know the whole of Waterloo for weeks, but I've lost some friends. I'll have to grieve a little."

He fell quiet for a moment. He was obviously deciding how much to tell her.

"It was close run. Wellington said as much. And close run to the very end. The officers, friends of mine, suffered heavy casualties. Old Hook is said to be . . . well, he never exhibits his feelings, but he's damned cut up. Evidently, Boney wasn't his old self. He made mistakes, and the duke took advantage. But God knows what would've happened if the Tyrant had been up to snuff. He's damnably brilliant. No matter what else, we have to give him that."

Again Max fell silent. He regathered himself, and yet again, he went on. "But it all certainly served to set me to rights. I've discovered what's important. And dangling after a rich wife isn't important to me. Oh, don't take me amiss. It would be easier to do what I need to do with a rich wife—or rather, with her fortune. But it's not in me to do it that way. So, I'm off to Bowwood. On my own. That, too, will be a close-run thing." His smile was his most soft. It was also typically Max. It warmed Lissa through the shadows. "The final irony is that Bagley's the one who'll tie the knot."

Lissa was surprised. "Your batman?"

"It seems he's also gone courting. Only he's been

successful. Both he and his wife are throwing in with me and leaving for Derbyshire."

"How wonderful. I'm happy for him."

"He's happy, too. A different fellow, in fact. It's nice to see. Naturally, you and Aggie can stay on here in town for as long as you like."

"When I close up, I'll send what remains of the staff to Bowwood," she reassured him. "But I don't think many will leave London. City servants don't usually go to the country. They feel demoted. Pinkerton, however, will stay on, I'm sure. Once the knocker is down, you'll need someone to watch the house."

To think that Westmane House would be closed up seemed strange. Sentiment crowded in. Lissa's thoughts of vacating the old place were almost incomprehensible.

But Max was smiling again, even if softly. "At least Waterloo diverted the talk from my ridiculous doings here of late."

"No more than a nine-day wonder," Lissa said dismissively.

"Yes," he said, on a masculine sigh. "What's before me seems easy after the rest." And then again, his mood shifted. He peered at her through the dim light. Their hands rested close on the handrail of the balustrade. "You've won our wager, you know. You must name your spoils."

Lissa chuckled. "I wouldn't know what to ask of you. Let's just call it—"

"No, no. That would go against the grain. Think of something you want. I'll bring it along with my wedding wishes. You're to be married in the country?"

Now Lissa experienced a softer turn of mood. "Yes. Will you give me away?"

"If I must."

She wanted desperately to change the subject. "After the ceremony, Aggie is off on a trip, you know."

"No, I didn't know."

"To the Lakes for the summer. With her friend, Aurora Maypost. Mrs. Maypost is the lady Aggie's been visiting, the one who's been ill . . ."

"Yes, yes, I recollect."

"Well, they're finally off on their own. They've been wanting to travel for years."

"Off on an adventure, eh?" he inquired, the light back in his eyes. "Well, Aggie has some money left. It should see her through a bit of travel now and again."

"Oh, no. It's Boysen's gift. He's very generous with Aggie, you know."

Max stiffened. "I'm glad for that."

"I'm sorry about the way he spoke to you at the Rodney ball."

Once again, Max sighed. "We'll never see eye to eye, Palmer and I. It's just as well there won't be much contact. Still, I hope you and I can remain friends. I recall saying that if we couldn't be cousins, I hoped we'd be friends. And now, I mean that doubly."

Lissa's heart plummeted. He continued to see them in the light of friendship, while she deeply loved everything about him. It was indeed best if they went their separate ways.

That they had been speaking for some time, that she should return to the guests who were talking in the chamber behind them, niggled at Lissa. Still, she wouldn't have much more time with Max. Surely they should enjoy what they'd have without guilt, without worrying about what someone might notice.

"Perhaps," she said to draw his eyes to her wry smile, "you'll find Mad Jack's treasure."

That served the purpose. He chuckled as readily as always. "I'll certainly be looking for it, my girl."

"And you'll be nice when you come to Boysen's seat to give me away?"

"I'll come with bells on."

They smiled at each other. Something bittersweet bound them together. They were saying goodbye.

"May I kiss you one last time?" he whispered, surprising her. Yes, he also felt the poignancy of parting.

"You may kiss me in the country. When I'm a bride."

"No," he said, still softly but seriously. "I'll not kiss you as a bride, Damalis."

She gathered herself. "You'll not kiss me on this balcony for all to see, either."

"My, my, you are a spoilt sport. And here, I've always thought you a great gun."

Once again, their eyes held. Lissa watched as Max's gaze drifted to her mouth. Boysen's voice stunned her into reality.

"I thought I'd find the pair of you closeted together." Palmer's figure was contrasted as a stiff silhouette against the light of the room behind him.

"Truly, Boysen," Lissa said. "We were discussing what's to be done with the house and servants."

"Any discussions," he said, turning on her with quick, quiet words, "can be had in the presence of either Lady Agatha or myself. This is too bad of you, Lissa."

Max's eyes drilled into Boysen's. "Let me ask you a question, Lord Palmer."

Boysen stiffened. "If you must."

"Do you love Damalis?"

Boysen couldn't have looked more startled if Max had struck him. "I say—"

"Just answer that one question. It's a simple one. Do you love Damalis?"

Lissa thought surely her betrothed wouldn't answer. But then, straightening his shoulders even more, he did. "I'm quite fond—"

"No," Max insisted. "I'm not speaking of fondness or affection. I've seen for myself that you don't respect her. What I'm asking is, do you love her?"

"I don't believe in the more passionate emotions. As everyone knows, they are unseemly."

"That's what I thought," Max said. "And on that count, coupled with the fact that I am head of Damalis's family, I must call off the engagement."

This time Boysen's comment almost reached the ears of those in the nearby room. "I beg your pardon," he barked. His pale complexion showed flushed, even in the dappled light.

"You heard me," Max said. "We're crying off."

"Why, I never—" Boysen stopped, only to collect himself and plunge ahead, his tones raspy. "Lissa's well beyond the age of permission. You're no more her guardian, her family, than you claim to be. She doesn't need your approval. We didn't ask for it in the first instance, nor are we seeking it now."

"Well, my girl," Max said, turning to Lissa, his eyes looking into hers. "I suppose I must give him that point. It's yours to decide. I depend on your wisdom."

Lissa's heart raced. So did her thoughts. Here, here, was an unheard of circumstance, an unlikely opportunity. And Max had prepared the way for it. She would never have considered crying off. If only she could call up the courage. And then, it came to her. That whispered bit she'd been holding onto ever since the night Max had kissed her in the windowseat in her bedchamber in the Thring country house.

He'd kissed her, or rather, coaxed her into kissing him. And then, he'd gotten up. He'd left. Even so, he'd said it. She was sure. "My love," he'd said, although she recalled nothing else. "My love." Maybe there was a chance for them. Maybe Max was forcing that chance.

Looking Boysen in the eyes, Lissa spoke as carefully and as considerately as she could. She and Boysen had been friends for a long time, but she could never love the man who stared at her. "Lord Palmer," she said, "I do beg your pardon, but I cannot marry you. I realize the great honor you've paid me, both in your friendship and in your proposal. But when considering our feelings, perhaps, they aren't enough. Not enough to hold us together through the many years to come. I hope you'll extend my deepest apologies to your kind mother. Indeed, I hope, my dear Boysen, that someday you'll find it in your heart to forgive me."

Lord Palmer simply stared for a moment. Because the light remained at his back, Lissa couldn't see him clearly. She thought he might say something. But then he turned as if to leave. Max's voice held him as surely as if he'd put a hand to his sleeve. "The ring, Damalis. You've forgotten that deuced ring."

Fortunately, the great ghastly ring that had been Boysen's mama's slipped off Lissa's finger easily. It had never belonged there, and she laid it just as readily onto the open palm of his hand. Bowing slightly, he looked at Max. "I would only add, Westmane, that you will see the ladies home, if you please. I, unfortunately, must leave."

Max paid his lordship the honor of replying in kind. "I shall be most happy to see my family home, my lord. Indeed, my family and I wish you nothing but well."

With a final bow, Lord Palmer left the balcony. The streets were momentarily quiet, but Lissa felt shaken. "I hoped that if anything would carry him through, it would be the amenities. Boysen always knows how to act when the proprieties are observed."

"I'm glad you had the presence of mind to think that clearly. I was about to land him a facer."

Lissa didn't know whether to laugh or cry. Her expectations of this wonderful man who stood beside her riveted her. Max.

At the moment, his look to her was anything but loverlike. Her heart thudded. "I suppose," he said, "there will be a furor."

"Absolutely. Our reputations will be in shreds. I'll be labeled jilt, and you fast and penniless."

And then, he was gathering himself again. He had great reserves. "Given time, those are labels we can live down. And," he added, finally looking at her, "you need not worry. I'll set it to rights. We go to the country as soon as may be. How soon, in fact, can you be ready?"

Lissa's thoughts scrambled. She tried to catch up with him, tried to ignore the subject she'd hoped they would broach. "A day or two should suffice. We've been packing up for weeks."

"And," he added with even more definition, "I'll find you a husband, as well. I have friends who'll be filtering back to England as soon as Bonaparte is run to ground. I'll set my mind to the proper one, and we'll invite him to Bowwood. Don't worry, my girl. We'll come about."

Lissa grasped for composure. Her thoughts spiraled. Had she thrown it all over for this? She'd turned her back on every effort she'd made at getting herself and Aggie off his hands. She'd taken one grand chance. She'd made one final leap for happiness. And now, Max was saying he'd find a husband for her among his friends.

She must have been mad. If he'd said, "my love," on that

night—which she now had to heartily doubt—he'd said it merely as a friend. It was all coming clear. Her frail hope had landed her in a final misery. Max was to be her matchmaker.

ℒ *Chapter Sixteen*

BOWWOOD. The seat of the Westmanes was a great rambling pile, verging on a romantic ruin. When they'd driven up the overgrown passageway, Lissa had first been impressed by its mellowed grandness. From its west end—a baron's hall begun in 1340—to its final easterly range, its broken rooflines, and especially its windows, told its story. Stone tracery openings in the chapel gave way to enormous Elizabethan lights. These in their turn surrendered to the march of early Georgian casements.

Bowwood claimed one of the first classical loggias to be built in England. The house had undergone extensive additions and numerous alterations, almost as regularly as the succession had passed from one hand to the next. It was fanciful. It was ponderous. There wasn't a single horizontal line from one wall to the next. And yet, it was all tied together in the same mellow stone that had been quarried by each generation from the same pit on the estate.

The park was forlorn, the gardens overgrown. To think of the tenantry made Lissa feel a combination of pity and guilt. There was hardly a vegetable in the kitchens, and the grand apartments, like the lesser rooms, were thick with dust.

Still, it wasn't tumbled-down. Instead it had more the sense of being benighted. It stood as it had been abandoned—left to the track of time. While it would always be worthy of a duke, it paid no tribute to the present one. It was altogether daunting and a great hodgepodge, but worst of all, it was in need of immediate attention. On this morning alone, a mere nine days after coming to Bowwood, they'd found two ceilings down on the upper floor.

Aggie, who'd been sorting through some papers Lissa had unearthed in the desk in the housekeeper's parlor, had dozed off in a sunny window in yet another parlor. Puck, too, had fallen victim to the same summer warmth, and Lissa let herself quietly out of the single room they'd straightened for their daily use. There was so much to be done, and she would love doing it. Her hands fairly itched. Still, she didn't know if she should. She didn't know where she stood. Max treated her more like a guest than family.

Making her way down through the big house, she was struck again by the vast differences between the two major Westmane houses. And yet the manses had similarities, too. Leaving the one had been a sad departure, but arriving at the other had been sadly like coming home. This was a painful conclusion for someone who knew she'd be allowed at Bowwood only temporarily. Daily, Max spoke of either this old comrade or that one. He told Lissa how grand they were—how they were following Boney to Paris, how they would all, God willing, come home soon. Lissa was heartily sick of it. It was as if he couldn't wait to be rid of her.

Turning down the center staircase in the antique structure, much as one would the grand stairs at Westmane House, Lissa was confronted by the great center hall. Here, a two-story structure with open beams and carved supports, with a ponderous chimneypiece and a scattering of tapestry-covered chairs, spoke only of Bowwood. Still, this entry space reminded her of the London house, as well. Fully armored warriors recalled the gladiator, the very thing she missed most of all. The Roman warrior had been her especial friend since childhood.

When she reached the stone flagging of the floor, she paused to peer up at the walls. They were covered by a mix of even more armory, by deer antlers collected from the park down through the decades, by portraits of her own ancestors. Ancestors with Titian-colored hair. Here were the very roots of the Westmanes. Here, long ago, Max's own beginnings had threaded through. Today, those gossamer threads tied Max to Bowwood as surely as if they were chains.

Lissa wondered if the responsibilities that had fallen on him were crushing him. Was it the newer burdens that set him at such a distance from her? All the while she longed to comfort him, to share the life he'd been forced into, she was thinking he'd do anything to get rid of her.

All she wanted was here, and Max.

On passing the library, Lissa peeked in. She hoped to see him. He was usually either in here, bent over the desk, or out riding Pegasus over the estate. But no. The chair at the desk was vacant, and the glass door was open. Outside it was a lovely day. A breeze invaded the house, coaxing the dust from the draperies, while rattling in the overhanging oaks outside.

Just beyond and up a slightly rising slope, Lissa saw Max. He was seated on the pair of steps that ran the circle of the rotunda. Mad Jack's rotunda. Tradition had it that it was here, to this white, wedding cake structure, that the mad duke had often brought his chair. He'd gone out to gloat over the treasure he'd buried, piece by piece, deep in the surrounding slopes.

But Max didn't appear to be interested in the treasure. Nor, for all its charm, was he interested in the rotunda. The open air folly was no more than a dome supported by a round of doric columns. The floor was flat and empty, open to the winds and rains. And while some Italianate stuccowork adorned the outer rim, the inside was plain. Plain, that was, except for the worn gilt letterings. " 'Tis here, 'tis there, 'tis everywhere. Thither and yon. Thither and yon," ran as a mockery, not once, but twice.

The newest Duke of Westmane, sitting casually on the steps, looked as if he belonged there. Lissa was growing accustomed to seeing him in shirt sleeves and with his hair ruffled, and thus he lounged today, his eyes intent on his small copy of the *Agamemnon*.

Coming up on him, across the recently scythed grass, Lissa thought he couldn't have appeared more charming, more intense, more . . . aloof.

"Good morning, Your Grace," she said.

The breeze fluttered her plain white muslin gown that was banded above the waist with no more than a blue ribband.

Max glanced up and smiled at her, rather in spite of himself than willingly. "You look a treat," he said. "Even with that smudge on your nose."

Lissa rubbed at her nose. "I'm fortunate it's only a smudge. I've been snooping around in the housekeeper's desk."

"I've told you not to put yourself out."

"I'm not. It's fascinating to poke around here. And I think it's also just as well the Hopkins are gone. He was no more a caretaker than she a housekeeper. Mrs. Bagley will do much better. She's as enthused to set to work as the rest of us."

He smiled at her, cryptically for Max.

He bent his head back to his Greek play, and she thought she'd been dismissed. She wouldn't give up that easily, however. She'd caught him unawares—neither busy with some ledger nor a tenant, and she saw her advantage. "Aggie's been going over the papers I found."

"She's not to worry," he said, not looking up. The breeze tugged at his chestnut hair. The sun exposed the lines of experience and masculinity in his dear, stubborn face.

Lissa plunged ahead. "Aggie's not so disappointed anymore. I mean, she's liking Bowwood better. Still, if she could I'm sure she would go to the Lakes this summer. If I didn't need to be chaperoned, she would."

"I'm sure she doesn't mind. She cares for you very much."

This time he didn't glance at her. In fact, he marked something into one of the margins of the small, worn volume with a pencil.

Lissa tried again. "I'm glad I found a position for Stowe and the vicar's wife has been very helpful in suggesting a girl from the village. Her name is Betsy. She's doing well. She's even managing this red mane of mine fairly well."

That brought up his reluctant gaze. Although it wasn't the fashion, Lissa knew Max liked it.

She pressed her advantage. "How are you doing with the translation?"

"A publisher in Oxford is thinking of printing it. Ollier has shown some interest, too."

"Max!" she exclaimed, surprised. "How wonderful!"

He shrugged a large shoulder, his eyes back to the book. "There won't be much money in it. I must admit I'm pleased, however. I was torn between calling it 'The Jameson Version' or 'The Westmane Version.' But I've decided on the latter. For good or ill, I'm Westmane, now."

This time his gaze lifted to drift over the enormous

structure that was his ducal seat. Yes. He was Westmane, now. Lissa saw, then, that he too liked Bowwood. She thought he liked it quite a bit. He'd said he'd wanted a home and, maybe, he felt as if he'd finally found it. Just as she felt.

Holding onto her courage, Lissa licked her lips. Her mouth felt dry and her knees shaky. Still, she stood her ground. He'd once told her that sometimes one had to throw one's heart over and follow it. "I've decided on what I want as my spoils. For the wager, I mean," she added nervously when he peered up at her, squinting his eyes against the sun behind her.

At last, he smiled. A little crookedly, but he smiled. "Oh? So what's it to be?"

"It might be more than—"

"Anything's fair. Winner names the spoils. That was the wager, and I lost. So, what's it to be?"

Memories of the night on the balcony, when she thought he would declare himself after Boysen's departure, tortured her. Still, the spoils was worth one bold strike at the heart of her golden-eyed enemy. "I should like to be the Duchess of Westmane."

For a moment she thought he might laugh, thinking to join her in a joke. But even as a smile tugged at the corners of his lips and barely lit his eyes, the lighter tack he would have taken failed. Without a word, he was scowling. Then, up on his feet. He left his little book carelessly behind and paced up, onto the empty floor of the rotunda. "You don't know what you're saying," he stated.

"Yes, I do," she said.

"I've been as much of a dreamer as Aggie to think I could put this place together without money. I might be able to do it on my own, but there's no guarantee. And it will certainly take me years and years to do so. To be the Duchess of Westmane is to be the duchess of a mare's nest."

"To be the Duchess of Westmane is all I can ask," she said stoutly, facing him squarely. "And so I've asked."

"I'm telling you that I didn't only find two ceilings down this morning—*before* breakfast, mind—but *after* breakfast, I discovered a mushroom growing in the dining room."

That salvo threatened to unhorse her. "A mushroom? Growing *in* the dining room?"

"Just so. Do you know what that means, ma'am?"

Since he stood now, his arms akimbo, his golden stare belligerent, she straightened her back and folded her arms over her own chest. "No, Your Grace. I don't know what finding a mushroom growing in the dining chamber has to do with my claim to my spoils."

"It means, ma'am, that the gutters have gotten blocked up. That means the rainwater has been diverted directly into the house. That, in its turn, means that some of the building has dry rot. Hence, the mushroom."

"Are you saying that you'll let a mushroom come between me and my winnings?"

"I'm saying that a mushroom in the dining room is indicative of precisely the mess I'm in. I'll not ask you to share that with me."

"And what about our wager? Everyone knows gentlemen pay their debts of honor above all else."

"Come now, Damalis. You're being nonsensical."

"You said you loved me," she blurted out.

His eyes shuttered. "Nonsense."

"Yes, you did. I heard you. That night at the Thrings, when you kissed me you said it."

"I wasn't thinking clearly that night."

"You said it," she announced. "Now, deny it."

"In any case," he said, his eyes softening, his arms dropping to his sides, "it was you who kissed me."

A silence fell between them. Lissa held her breath. She watched as Max moved down the steps toward her. She felt as if something had changed, but she couldn't read his gaze. Surely, something had changed.

Then he came right up to her and bent without touching her to speak in her ear. "All hail the conqueror. All hail the Duchess of Westmane."

Lissa waited until his gaze met hers. And then, his arms enfolded her tightly. He smiled at her as only Max could. His eyes danced. "So, you're to be my duchess, eh? Now I'll be able to 'Your Grace' you in the most odious manner. Now I shall kiss you as often as I want. And without looking for an excuse. That is," he added, the least wrinkle in his brow, "I'll kiss you only as often as you let me."

She took her turn to smile up at him. "Then, it will be as often as you like."

He grinned his pleasure. His lips touched hers, tentatively for Max. It was as if he wanted her to be sure. His embrace tightened. He was a wonderfully confident male at all the right times. Lissa was lost in visions of being his duchess—of being just like this, in his embrace no matter what disasters waited for them in the house or because of finances.

Suddenly, he swept her up in his arms under the domed ceiling of the rotunda. He spun her about, grinning gaily. "Mad Jack," he cried, "I've found my treasure! You can gloat no more!"

Breathless and slightly dizzy, Lissa laughed. "Max, let me down—I'll swoon."

"Swoon away," he whispered, "I'll always be here to catch you."

The ceiling spun over her head, the gilt letters whirling madly.

"Max, stop! Let me down! It's here!" Lissa suddenly yelled.

"What?" He let her slide to the ground, where she leaned dizzily against him.

"It's *here*. Have you ever thought of that precise pair of words? I mean, in the riddle. And stamped so directly into the dome."

Turning—with her still in the curve of his arms—Max peered up at the old gilt lettering that marched the inner round of the domed ceiling. "Tis here," he repeated. "By gad," he said, with definition. Walking to the edge of the rotunda, he hollered even more loudly, "Bagley! Bagley!"

A window on the second story scratched open. "Up here, Colonel! What's amiss?"

"Fetch my pistols. And the powder. And your Brown Bess. Any blunderbuss that'll fire."

Bagley sliced his eyes about, looking for the dastardly intruder.

"Step lively, man!"

"Aye, Colonel!" the fellow snapped back.

Max and Lissa walked the small round of the space then. The garden structure was soundly built, and their eyes and conjectures kept going back to the riddle in flaking, gilt letters. Soon, the stout batman was huffing and puffing up the slope. His arms were full of weapons that Lissa hadn't known were in the house.

"What's amiss, Colonel? Beggin' your pardon, miss."

"Just stand by and load, you old lay about." Lifting his pistol, Max spoke to Lissa. "Hold your ears, my love."

She obliged and he fired. And then he fired again. As fast as Bagley could load, Max fired his shot into the thick coatings of plaster. A few puffs of white dust resulted, and a great pall of blue smoke from the barrels. Indeed, Lissa couldn't believe the din, the fierce, red hot blasts each time a weapon discharged. Still, not much happened. Lissa was somewhat surprised when Max reverted to Bagley, excitement continuing to mark his golden eyes. "Into the great hall with me, old man. We'll have a whole assortment of equipment there."

Bagley peered at Max as if he'd run mad. Still, when Max left Lissa with a peck to her cheek and a promise of a quick return, the batman followed faithfully.

They were back in a wink, loaded down with the ancient instruments of war usually displayed with the standing suits of armor.

"Hand me the halbard," Max said to Bagley, while blessing Lissa with a grin. "I'll give it few good whacks, and you do the same with the pole arm. But be careful, old fellow."

"I can hit it as well as you, sir. And be as careful, too."

The pair begun, then, to beat at the curve of stucco. Great clouds of dust soon filled the air, while chunks of plaster fell on their heads. When the rain began, a veritable shining rain of gold coins, Max released a "Ho!" Just under the flaking gilt of the letters, a cubby-hole was revealed as the source for the flashing shower. Coins bounced and rang against the flooring, down the steps, and out onto the lawn.

"Billy be damned!" Bagley shouted when Max scooped up Lissa for another spin.

Grabbing a handful of coins that at last lay in a fog of drifting dust and white plaster, Max displayed them for her. "By Jove! Five-guinea pieces! With none other than George the Second on 'em, just as Aggie said."

As if he'd conjured her up, Aggie emerged from the house. She looked puzzled. Her red mane was never more askew, and Puck trotted at her heels. "My stars! Whatever is it? I'd thought it had begun to thunder something dreadful."

Lissa grabbed her aunt in a hug. "You were right."

"I? Right? Why, how can that be?"

"It's Mad Jack's treasure, my dear," Max called to her. He looked like a ghost. Plaster whitened his hair and his cheeks, his eyes showing through like eerie holes. Lissa was on the verge of laughing, when she gasped. "Max! There's another here."

The ladies stood by as yet second shower of gold coins was exposed after almost seventy years of being hidden away. And then, even before the last coins rained to the floor, Lissa spoke again. "Max. There's a cache in 'there.' And Max, there's—"

"By blood and thunder, yes!" he said. " 'Here' is 'everywhere.' Can it be possible?"

Yes, it was possible. Four more caches, six in all, were revealed as Bagley and Max made a mighty effort. Lissa and Aggie looked on, while Puck backed away, across the lawn, afraid of the noise. Indeed, it was an unlikely scene for man or beast. Plaster dust rose up like cotton wool to envelop the quaint structure.

"Who would have thought?" Max finally posed, once it was over and all seemed quiet. "Now it's our turn to laugh at old Mad Jack. Still, I give him credit. Who would have believed it?"

"I would have," Aggie piped. "If only my nurserymaid had known, I would have believed it in a minute."

They all laughed, and a nearly white Max caught Lissa up again, in this instance in waltz time. Across the lawn they swept, as gracefully as if in a ballroom. When Bagley plunked Puck into her ladyship's arms, Aggie pulled a knowing face at him. The batman, who was as free as her ladyship, pulled a face right back.

"I'm as rich as Croesus!" Max yelled. "I'm as rich as Golden Ball! I'm as rich as a Nabob! I'm as rich as love can make me!"

Surely, he was heard all the way to London. At all events, Lissa thought—with an excessive amount of satisfaction—London would soon hear. The new Westmane had finally come into his own. The *monde* would be agog.

From the *New York Times* bestselling author
of <u>Forgiving</u> and <u>Bitter Sweet</u>

LaVyrle Spencer

One of today's best-loved authors of bittersweet
human drama and captivating romance.

___THE ENDEARMENT	0-515-10396-9/$5.99
___SPRING FANCY	0-515-10122-2/$5.95
___YEARS	0-515-08489-1/$5.95
___SEPARATE BEDS	0-515-09037-9/$5.99
___HUMMINGBIRD	0-515-09160-X/$5.50
___A HEART SPEAKS	0-515-09039-5/$5.99
___THE GAMBLE	0-515-08901-X/$5.99
___VOWS	0-515-09477-3/$5.99
___THE HELLION	0-515-09951-1/$5.99
___TWICE LOVED	0-515-09065-4/$5.99
___MORNING GLORY	0-515-10263-6/$5.99
___BITTER SWEET	0-515-10521-X/$5.95